FUTURE-PROOF & COSY
Issue n° 12 — Winter 2018

PART 1

With cover star LAURIE ANDERSON, photographed by Mark Peckmezian in Copenhagen, Denmark.

PART 2

A consortium of monsters inspired by FRANKENSTEIN; OR, THE MODERN PROMETHEUS, a novel dreamt up by Mary Shelley in 1816 and published for the first time in 1818.

Every image in this issue, dismembered and then reassembled.

An image of proper
reading enthralment,
by CHRISTOPHER
ANDERSON.

SLOW DOWN

An underrated part of the reading experience is the time when you are not reading at all, those moments between sentences when the mind just wanders. During *Frankenstein*, you look out of the train window at the cables going past and think how far electricity has come, what a gratifying word 'electric' is, and how much you like the song 'Together in Electric Dreams', released in 1984, a year that was the title of... oh no, what am I doing? Read!

There's an argument that these digressions should be considered part of the reading process rather than separate from it. Reading is a mysterious activity: a kind of hallucinatory state, both vivid and frustratingly ephemeral. Whatever it is that we are utterly absorbed in will more often than not vanish from memory the moment it is set aside. Days after reading a book by a hilarious moth expert, you find yourself at a dinner party where everyone is talking about moths, and have nothing better to offer than, 'I just read a book about moths.' It had loomed so large, during the act. You were a moth expert too; the author's thoughts were your thoughts. Where did all the information go? Why even bother?

A book, apparently, is not an upload; a reader is not a computer. When a book finds its way into our long-term memory, it tends to do so via the actual senses. Decades later, we might still recall the thickness and colour of its cover, the atmosphere of its typeface, the place in which we read it, the emotional texture of our lives at the time of doing so. Just not the words; unless we somehow broke them out of their cell. The term is 'active reading'. Neuroscientists assert that by grappling with a book's contents, and not being temporary vessels for an author's compositions, we are carving out new neural pathways: connections are made, memories are formed, the book is actually becoming part of us. You could take notes, copy out passages, affix annotations, make associative diagrams, amass index cards, arrange collages, compose lyrics, trace character routes through cities, stand when a character stands and lie on the floor when they lie on the floor. But just pausing frequently to think also counts, and letting the associations (*The Happy Reader* is a lot to do with those associations) run their course.

THE HAPPY READER
Bookish Magazine
Issue n° 12 — Winter 2018

The Happy Reader is
a collaboration between
Penguin Books and
Fantastic Man

EDITOR-IN-CHIEF
Seb Emina

EDITORIAL DIRECTORS
Jop van Bennekom
Gert Jonkers

MANAGING EDITOR
Maria Bedford

DESIGN
Tom Etherington

DESIGN CONCEPT
Jop van Bennekom
Helios Capdevila

PICTURE RESEARCH
Samantha Johnson

PRODUCTION
Ilaria Rovera

PUBLISHER
Helen Conford

MARKETING DIRECTOR
Ingrid Matts

BRAND DIRECTOR
Sam Voulters

MANAGING DIRECTOR
Stefan McGrath

CONTRIBUTORS
Jeremy Allen, Geoff Dyer, Jean
Hannah Edelstein, Charlie Fox,
Jordan Kelly, Emily King, Jeffrey
Lewis, Jamie MacRae, Pascal-
Désir Maisonneuve, Yelena
Moskovich, Mark Peckmezian,
Justin E. H. Smith, Amelia Tait,
Lan Truong, Jan Erik Waider.

THANK YOU
Magnus Åkesson, Megan Conery,
Hernan Diaz, Rebecca Lee, Anna
Mercer, Michael Morris, Eric
Niiler, Aaron Peck, Caroline
Pretty, Fiona Sampson, Ida
Skovmand, Matthew Slotover,
Nadja Spiegelman, Antonia Webb,
Julie Woon, Matthew Young.

Penguin Books
80 Strand
London WC2R 0RL

info@thehappyreader.com
www.thehappyreader.com

SNIPPETS

Shocking gossip, rumour and sightings to keep up with goings-on in bookland.

GONZO — A car has written a book, sort of. Artificial intelligence creator Ross Goodwin installed a Cadillac with a camera, microphone, GPS unit, clock and AI writing machine, then took the car on a road trip from New York to New Orleans. The writing machine's resulting novel is entitled *1 the Road*, and opens with the following line: 'It was seven minutes to ten o'clock in the morning, and it was the only good thing that had happened.'

CITY LIT — Trans-national peace promoter UNESCO has named Kuala Lumpur as 2020's World Book Capital. The Malaysian capital will follow Athens, Greece (2018), and Sharjah, United Arab Emirates (2019), as the most important, or most promoted-by-the-UN, readerly city in the world. Excellent KL bookshops include Silverfish (indie), Projek Rabak (arty) and Kinokuniya (huge).

RACY — Finnish Formula One racer Kimi Räikkönen has released a book of haiku.

HERO — John Kennedy, owner of one of the oldest bookshops in south London, has died. The bookselling legend, instantly recognisable thanks to his long white beard, founded East Dulwich's Chener Books in 1978 and never particularly changed it after that. 'We're old-fashioned,' he told *The Dulwich Diverter* in 2016. 'We haven't really got into the twenty-first century yet. They should have extended the twentieth century.' The shop, happily, remains open.

BREAKBEAT — A man in a white T-shirt made headlines for the simple act of reading John Berger's *Ways of Seeing* at a drum 'n' bass rave. Jono Hope, twenty-eight, bought the seminal work of art criticism en route to the blowout in Bristol, UK, and was filmed reading it on a metal staircase, a stark contrast with the heaving mass of bodies below. 'I just wanted a few minutes away from the madness,' he said. 'Security guards kept coming up to me and asking to sift through the book to check there were no drugs in there.'

STAMP — Public libraries in the USA are getting to be so pragmatically imaginative about what they offer for checkout. Books are available, of course. Music and DVDs, sure! But in Lickey County, Ohio, libraries will lend their patrons acoustic guitars, while in New York and Philadelphia, a cardholder can borrow a necktie and briefcase if they are feeling under-wardrobed for a job interview.

LOVE — Scottish First Minister Nicola Sturgeon is perhaps the most bookish of all world leaders, and often refers to current books on her bedside table (a recent revelation was William Boyd's *Love is Blind*). At this year's Wigtown Book Festival, during a discussion about her lifelong reading habits, she named her favourite book as 1932's *Sunset Song*, by quintessential Scottish writer Lewis Grassic Gibbon.

PACKAGING — When Gemma Janes, a British expat in Paris, realised she had too many books to lug back to London, she decided to try to start a mail-order bookshop of sorts. At first she just posted shots of the books to Instagram, allowing people to pay whatever they wanted, but it has now mushroomed into a serious operation, Sendb00ks, with a different artist recruited each month to create an accompanying postcard. Former *Happy Reader* cover star Lily Cole even donated a bunch of her old reading matter to the project.

I DO — French author Michel Houellebecq, whose name is often preceded by the word 'controversial', married his partner Qianyum Lysis Li at a town hall in Paris. This was his third time getting married, and he wore a bowler hat. After the ceremony, a reception was held at Lapérouse, an old riverside restaurant that was formerly a regular haunt for literary greats such as Émile Zola, Victor Hugo and George Sand, and enjoyed a stint as a discreet if infamous high-class brothel. Houllebecq led the karaoke with a rendition of Françoise Hardy's 'Tous les garçons et les filles'.

RAFFLE — A Dutchman living in Wales won a bookshop in a raffle. After deciding to retire due to poor health, Paul Morris, proprietor of Bookends in Cardigan, decided to give the shop to one of his dedicated customers. The winner, Ceisjan van Heerden, was handed the keys and is now running the popular (and, it should be noted, profitable) literary business.

LAURIE ANDERSON

In conversation with
EMILY KING

Portraits by
MARK PECKMEZIAN

Laurie Anderson is an artist, composer, film-maker, poet, morning person and improbable pop star. She lives in New York, and loves to read. Her work often features books: there have been songs about William Faulkner's porch, Russian novels shredded and repurposed as cinema screens, and an operatic adaptation of *Moby Dick*. In a gallery in Denmark where she's making a new computer-constructed reality, *The Happy Reader* interviews the world's most atypical celebrity.

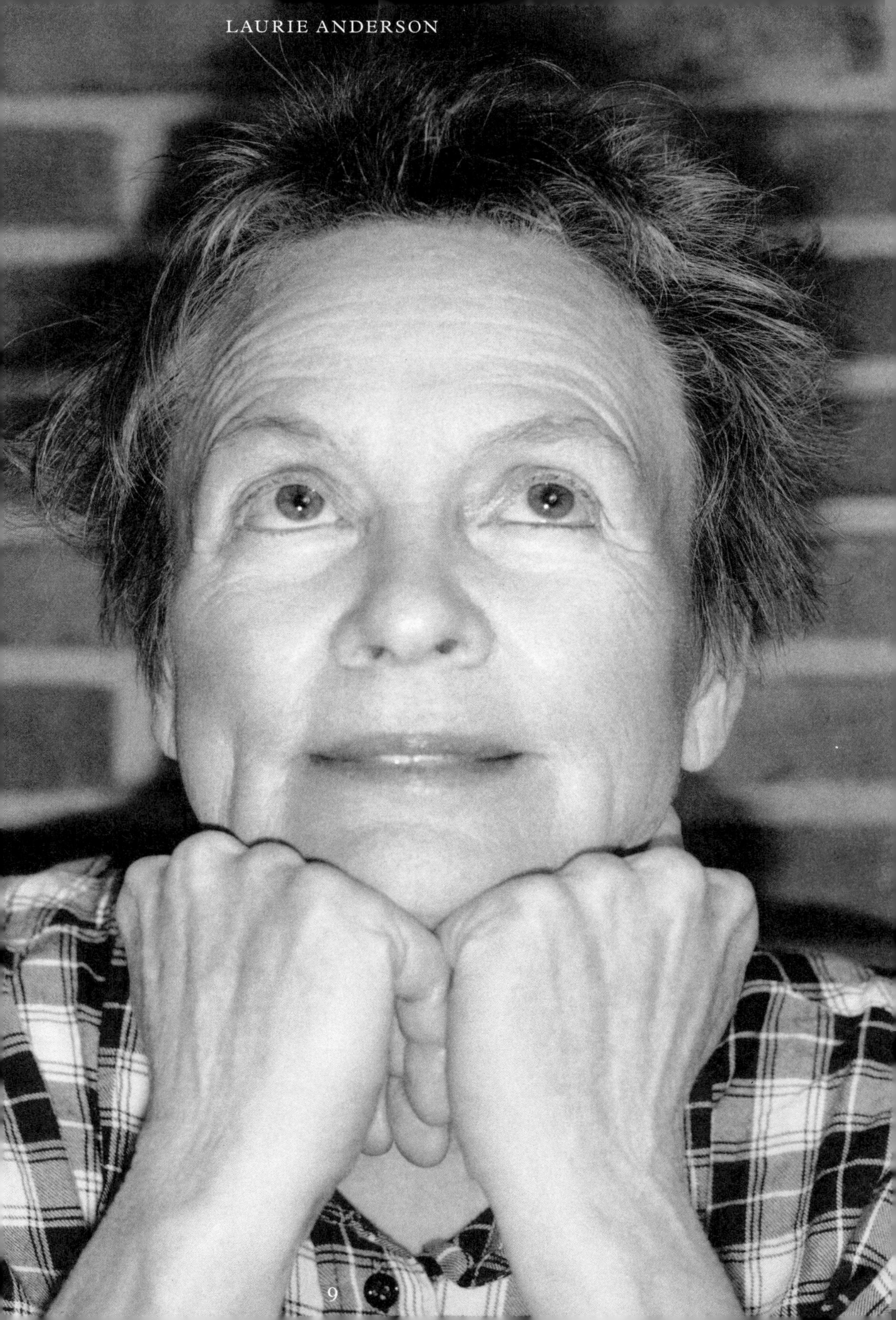

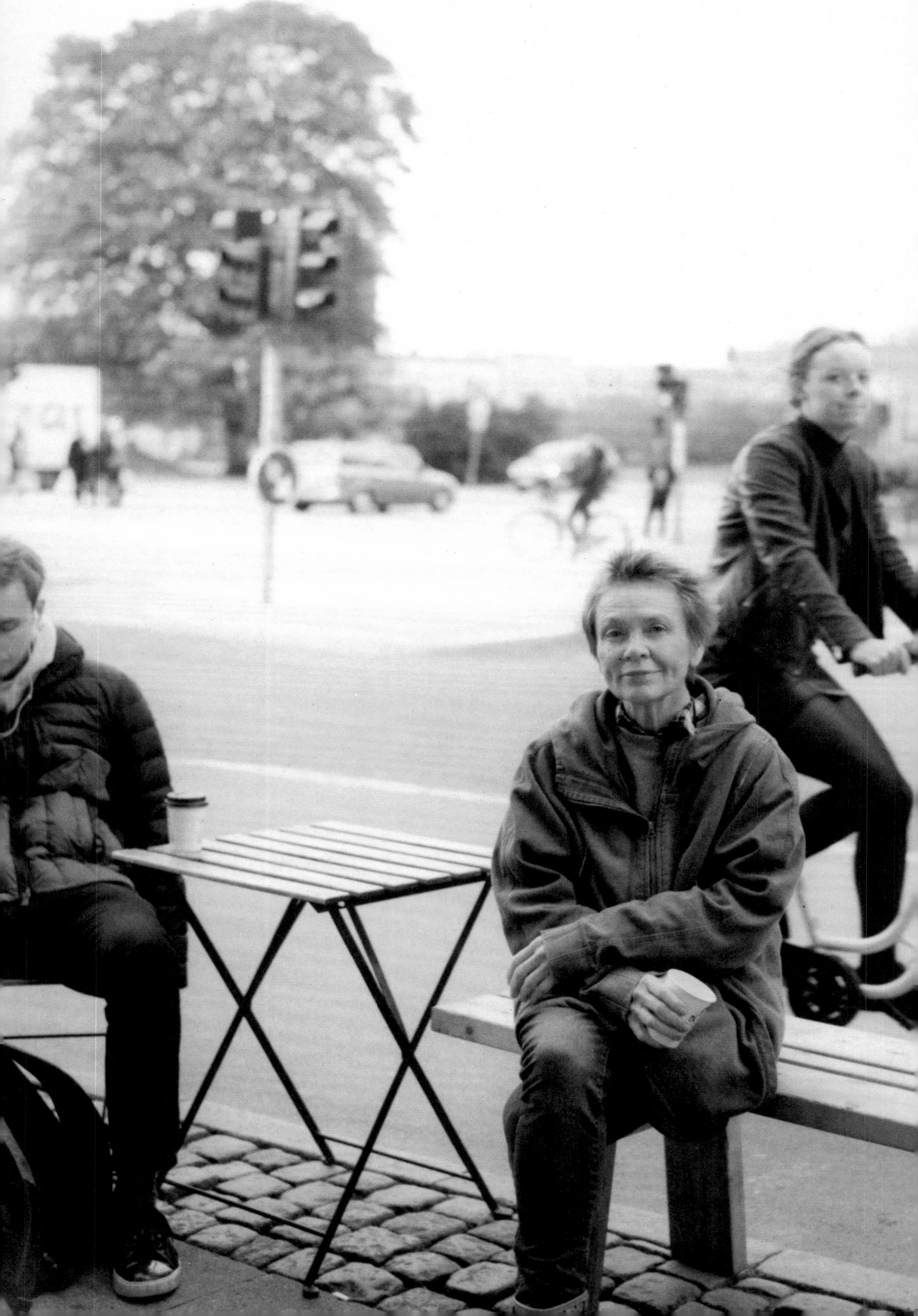

HUMLEBÆK

It's a damp September day in Copenhagen. Communicating by text, Laurie Anderson and I agree to meet at noon at the Louisiana, a museum of modern art forty kilometres north of Copenhagen by the Øresund, the strait between Denmark and Sweden. She is installing a new virtual reality piece made in collaboration with the Taiwanese artist Hsin-Chien Huang. Putting participants in an imagined moonscape, it is part of the museum's expansive temporary exhibition about the cultural and scientific framing of the earth's moon.

Laurie was co-opted into pop culture when her 1981 song 'O Superman' reached number 2 in the UK singles chart. While the song is immediate and addictive, the resulting fame seemed unlikely. Laurie was and is a determinedly avant garde artist and performer whose multidisciplinary work plays with the fringes of the humanly and technologically possible. Her long relationship with Lou Reed cemented her place as a musical celebrity, but that status never affected her fabulously experimental agenda. On my arrival, Laurie is engaged in a conversational millefeuille with the programming team who are finessing the details, with a gallery technician who is hanging a translucent curtain, and with gallery attendants who will guide the audience through the VR experience. In part to get me out of the way, I am helped into a headset and backpack and spend ten minutes in gleeful orbit, my favourite part astride some kind of lunar mule. I emerge to hear Laurie telling the story of the Russian philosopher Nikolai Fedorov (1829–1903), who is sometimes called 'the father of space travel'. Fedorov wanted to tour the galaxy in order to retrieve the scattered dust of the dead and reconstitute it into living bodies.

Still woolly-legged from my trip, I follow Laurie to the Louisiana's staff canteen where I just about manage to monopolise her attention over lunch. Following up on the extraordinary Fedorov, we head straight into a conversation about her favourite books.

EMILY: Fedorov's theories are wild. Where on earth did they come from, exactly?

LAURIE: I've read a lot of things that were written around Fedorov's time — Karl Marx, for instance. I like books that are written in the same year, but take a very different turn. An example: *The Communist Manifesto* and *Bartleby, the Scrivener* were written just a short period of time apart. They're both about work, but one is this giant billboard — 'Workers of the World, Unite!' — and then *Bartleby, the Scrivener*, on the other side, is a guy who would rather not work!

E: That's the 'I prefer not to' story?

    L: Yeah, it takes you to self-annihilation, that preference. It's no joke. Marx is a wonderful book to read now because it's a ghost story: 'A spectre is haunting Europe.' That spectre is back, and why we work is even more mysterious, and how we feel about work, and how we feel about losing our jobs. And I love mythical stories: *His Dark Materials*.

E: Oh yeah, Philip Pullman.

    L: Big fan.

E: Me too.

    L: Because it makes it possible to be twelve again.

E: .What did you read when you were twelve?

    L: Oh, let's see. In the movie that I did called *Heart of a Dog*...

E: I actually watched that last night.

    L: Oh, OK! So, you know there's a story about reading, or being read to, in hospital after I had broken my back, when I was twelve. *The Little Grey Rabbit*: it literally was torture. I had been reading books like *Crime and Punishment* and *A Tale of Two Cities*.

E: You were reading *Crime and Punishment* at twelve!

    L: Yes.

E: That's quite precocious.

    L: It's pretentious maybe.

E: No, ambitious.

    L: When I was in, maybe, fourth or fifth grade, I would carry a big stack of books like this [gestures in front of her]. It was almost a wall in front of me, my eyes just peeping over. I'd be reading them, of course, but what I liked the most was the barrier.

E: Was your mother a reader?

    L: Yes. She was a lot of things. She graduated from University of Chicago when she was sixteen, so she was really very bright, but then proceeded to have eight kids, so she had to read at night. Some of my earliest memories are of getting up very early, four in the morning, and finding her still up, reading.

E: What was she reading?

L: All kinds of things. Philosophy, particularly philosophy. For me, reading was how I got out of raking leaves. I didn't have to do what the other kids did, because I was doing that.

E: It was a source of respect in your family?

L: Not just respect, veneration. It was like: 'You're reading? Wow! You're doing something very, very important.'

E: Where did you find books?

L: The library, where everyone found them. I liked to browse. I liked to chatter with my teachers. I was the kind of person that came to school so early that no one else was there. Brown-nosing my teachers, beating the fish, racing the board, asking, 'What is this new book?' They were all really helpful. The first time I visited the Louisiana, Knud, who was the first director here, he was in his sixties or seventies at that time, and he lived here in the big house, and we just sat in the library and talked about books. We sat there till the end of the day. Who does that any more? No one. Ever. Does that. If I could say one thing in whatever we're doing here, it's that I want so much to try to bring that feeling of luxuriousness, of talking and reading.

E: I think we don't know when to read any more. We feel like we don't have time.

L: I totally feel that. I solved it by alternating mornings. I either get up and do t'ai chi and meditate, or I stay in bed, get a coffee and read for two or three hours, from 5.30 to 8.30. It's a great time. Really cosy. It depends on the weather, it depends on my energy, it depends on my interests. But for me that's the best time to read. That's the best time to do anything, really.

E: Do you read through the rest of the day?

L: Any time that I can. I bring books with me everywhere I go.

E: Have you got a book with you now?

L: I have a Kindle and I'm reading some James Lee Burke. I found an old Kindle of Lou's, and I have to read everything on it. It's from about 2013, so I've read martial arts books, and James Lee Burke, and how-to-take-care-of-your-heart books.

E: A nice mix.

L: Curated by Lou, just like a present for me. Otherwise I'm reading a book by Sjón, an Icelandic writer, called *CoDex 1962*. It just came out. I'm doing an event at the New York Public Library with

2. 5.30

Other notable 5.30am risers include:
– Maya Angelou, writer
– Jack Dorsey, entrepreneur
– Peter Eisenman, architect
– Marco Sullivan, alpine skier
– Ivanka Trump

3. LOU'S

Lou Reed's first taste of fame was during the 1960s as frontman for a rock band with a name stolen from a book. Published in 1963, *The Velvet Underground* by Michael Leigh was about 'the sexual corruption of our age.'

him. Speaking of which, I'm really inspired by libraries taking over some of the empty space that is left where there used to be dialogue. In the old days, we used to have a liberal left-wing of intellectuals and writers, and we don't have that any more. We don't have Susan Sontag any more, and that really is painful. It's really painful not to have writers who are speaking up. Very, very precious few. *CoDex 1962* is a kind of lovely fantasy. It's very long, it's complicated and full of fantasy. I read to come down late at night, and late at night here is 4 a.m., because we're so busy installing this piece.

E: Is it fiction?

L: Yes. They asked me and Sjón to do an event at the Black Diamond Library in Copenhagen about a year and a half ago. It was supposed to be about climate — Sjón knows much more than I do about that. Right now the trend is to ask artists and writers to talk about climate, because it's on everybody's mind. Sjón spent six months at a climate institute, so he's very up to speed about what's going on, but I'm not like that. We decided to talk about it anyway because it's another way to talk about story structure, because everyone has a story about where things are going now. Many people's story is apocalypse: the story that gets darker and darker until we run out of food and water and air and ocean and... Both Sjón and I agreed that that's a story that is impossible to tell, in public anyway...

E: The story of the apocalypse?

L: Well, extinction let's say. It's not that we're moving into the sixth extinction. We're in it. It's not something you can reverse. If you think the fire starters of technology are going to rush in and fix up the ozone hole, you're out of your mind. That's not going to happen. You just see where this is going, and I feel an obligation to talk about it, and not to deflect it or go somewhere else with it. But it's not a story you can tell in public because: 'OK, so we're wiped off the face of the planet.' We will be, undoubtedly, and we see it coming, but people don't want to hear it.

E: It makes me think of that novel, *The Road*. You know, by the man who wrote about cowboys.

L: Oh yeah. Cormac McCarthy.

E: There's something about that story: from the start, it can't pan out any other way, but still you're driven to read it to the end.

L: It's a road, and a road is always a good metaphor for a plot. But in the case of extinction, you're telling the story to who? To no one. And that is an awesome thing. You tell a story, usually you think of your reader, or even speaking to history, abstract history. In this case, you're speaking to no one. Sjón and I talk about that a lot. What is the story to tell? It's not a story people want to hear, because we're human, and people want to do something. They don't want to just sit there sliding into oblivion. That's not a story that anyone wants to hear. I still haven't decided what to do about that, because I think 'if you see something, say something'. There it is. You don't shut up about it just because it's unbelievably depressing. That story is one of absolutes, it's beyond abstention. I asked my Buddhist teacher about it. 'What happens to karma when there are no more people? How does that work? Where does that energy go?' And he had an answer: 'Well, that's why the Buddha talked about other universes.' Makes sense.

E: They're definitely there.

   L: You can go to them in your mind. You have a lot of power in that situation. But the world now works on fear. Everyone is frantically looking at their clocks all the time and their messages, and they're afraid. I try to look at what I am afraid of every day. I was just reading something this morning about a writer who talked about fear as a motivator. She just wrote a novel that I made a note to get immediately, but I haven't got it yet. The book begins with a Samuel Johnson quote, 'How small, of all that human hearts endure, that part which laws or kings can cause or cure.' How invested are you in what's going on with your king, or whatever? How much is it really affecting your life? Well, a lot right now.

E: Well, you're distracted by the relentless weird behaviour of your king, but I guess in your day-to-day existence it might not have such an impact... It's so depressing, isn't it?

   L: It's more than depressing.

E: It's brutalising.

   L: It's so bad: 'OK, arm the teachers!'

E: Can we talk more about your teachers?

   L: My teachers helped me a lot. One day, I got to school so early it was still closed. I started home, and when I saw people on their way to school, I said, 'Forget it, school is closed today.' They went, 'Really?' But they believed me, as an authority figure. 'It's closed!' They went home. And then, when I got home, my mother said, 'It's not closed, go back!' So I went back and got there just on time, but they were all late, all those people I'd given advice to. I'm a bit of a hysterical person, so when I'm talking about extinction... Arriving really early at school, I was very enveloped in time and I still am, really. I feel the

4. IF YOU SEE SOME-
THING, SAY SOMETHING
—
The US's vigilance-
promoting motto was
written after 11 Septem-
ber 2001 by an adver-
tising executive named
Allen Kay. Worldwide
equivalents include:
— 'If it doesn't add up,
   speak up.' (Australia)
— 'Watchful together.'
   (France)
— 'Be alert. Not alarmed.'
   (Hong Kong)
— 'See it. Say it. Sorted.'
   (UK)

5. SAMUEL JOHNSON
—
Johnson, who wrote the
original Dictionary of the
English Language (1755),
once declined an invita-
tion to go backstage at
a theatre like this: 'The
silk stockings and white
bosoms of your actresses
excite my amorous
propensities.'

Laurie, currently practising the martial art of tai chi, is photographed here and throughout in the snug city of Copenhagen.

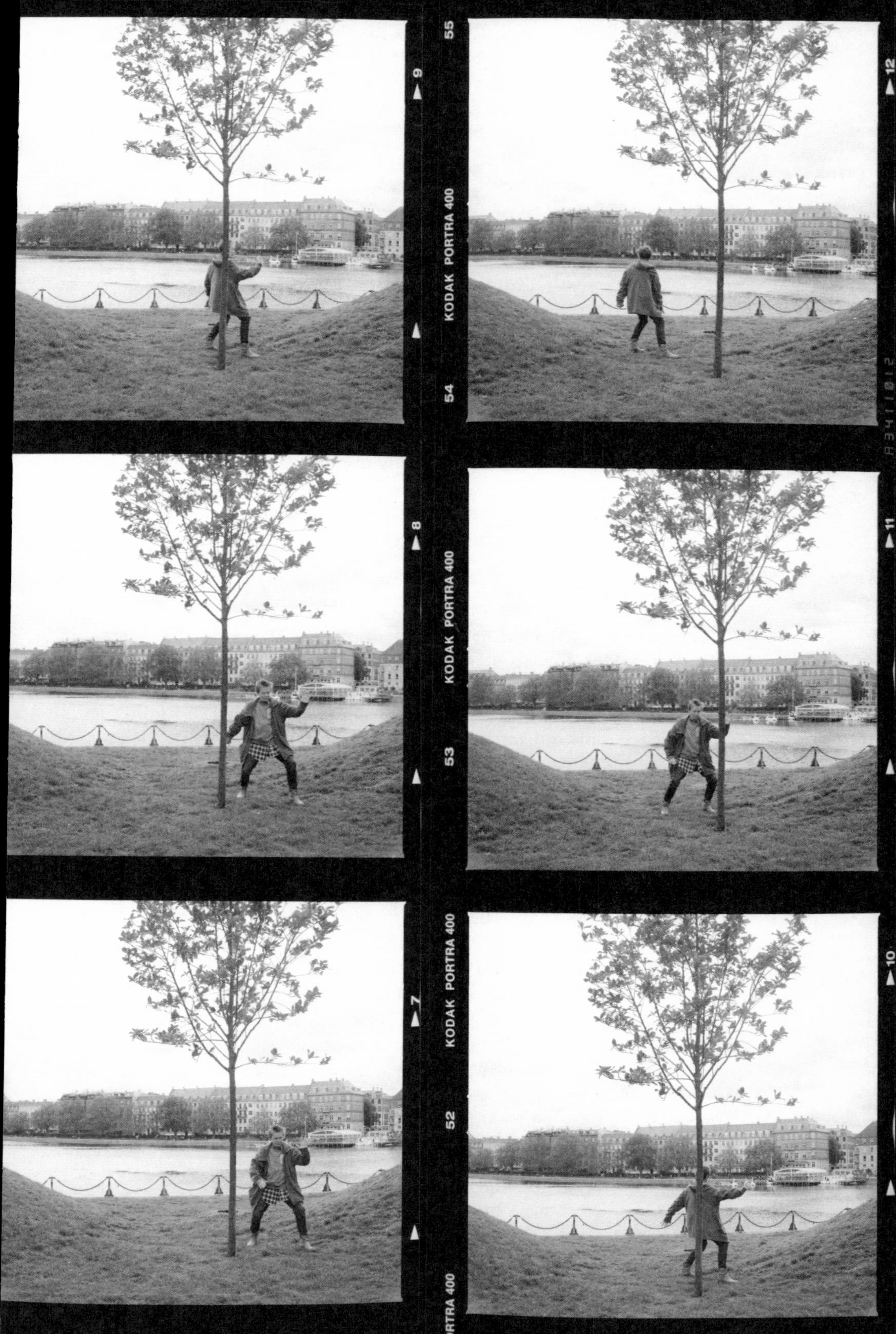
9
KODAK PORTRA 400
55
54
12
8
KODAK PORTRA 400
53
11
7
KODAK PORTRA 400
52
10
RTRA 400

crunch of time, I feel it. When I dive into a really long book, it feels wonderful to counteract that fear of losing time, because you're going to live in the book for a while. Everything I've made has been about disembodiment, which is why virtual reality is really interesting to me. But you can get just as disembodied in a book or you can lose yourself just as much in a pencil drawing. VR has nothing better or worse in terms of making that happen. And that's always my goal, to lose myself.

E: Do you see a big distinction between fiction and non-fiction?

L: It's really unimportant to me. I feel that's sort of a corporate question, in that, when I was at Warner Brothers, they were constantly going, 'Are you a pop artist, or an avant-garde artist, or electronic artist, or what are you?' It was only to decide which bin to put the record in. Otherwise, who cares? I mean, 'Is it good or not?' As soon as the record industry collapsed, no one cared what category you were in and you were free to make really weird records. Not to say there aren't pop records, there certainly are.

E: I am of the British generation that first heard of you through 'O Superman', which came at me as a pop record, though it clearly is not. But it kind of is.

L: It kind of is.

E: If I start 'Ha ha ha', everyone around me will sing, 'O, Superma-an.'

L: I have to sing that song in a couple of days with a choir all going 'Ha ha ha'. I haven't done that in a very long time. I'm not someone who does hits, I don't have a hit show, although I am going to put together some old songs for something I'm doing later in the month.

E: Back to the categories: it doesn't make a difference if something is explicitly fiction, or if it's purporting to be fact?

L: I'm not cutting it that way. So much of science is speculation to start with, or so unbelievably fabulous, and fiction can be so prosaic and dreary. So, maybe I draw the line between interesting and dreary, rather than true or not true. I've never been that interested in whether things are literally happening to you or not. I think we're much more empathetic than that, and if someone tells you a really powerful story, it can feel as though it happened to you. Now, if you present it as your own, that can be a problem. You have to recognise that it's empathy with another, not your own experience. That is very different. For example, a friend of mine told me that his ninety-year-old mother had a really good solution for leaving dinner parties, because she didn't like them at all. She would come up to the hostess at the beginning of the party and say, 'I have to leave at nine' in this very conspiratorial voice. And, because it's a secret, instead of saying, 'But dinner is at eight! Why are you leaving at nine?', the hostess says, 'Oh, I will get you out the door.' I thought that is genius, so I tried it a bunch of times and it worked perfectly. Then I was telling this friend, 'You know, a friend of mine told me a story about his mother who got out of dinner parties' and he said, 'I told you that story.' At least I didn't claim it was my mother!

6. GRAVITY'S RAINBOW

Laurie's 1984 song 'Gravity's Angel' was inspired by Pynchon's legendarily difficult novel.

E: And at least you didn't try the trick on him either!

L: Exactly. So, I think stories flow, and the wonderful thing is that you recognise them because we're very similar in so many ways. When you tap into something that other people feel in the same way as you, it is so exciting. It's not about inventing something for me, it never has been. It's about tapping into something in someone else and them going, 'God, I know what you're talking about, I just didn't put it into those words!' It's not some weird image with tentacles that's so interesting and surrealistic that no one even dreamed it existed, it's something that makes people say, 'Oh wow! I know how that feels!'

E: Do you think there's something about books having a single author, something that makes them the most direct way of accessing someone else's thoughts?

L: Maybe. Maybe it depends on the book. In many of my favourite books, I'm totally Slothrop, I'm totally some character in the book.

E: Slothrop?

L: You know, Thomas Pynchon, *Gravity's Rainbow*.

E: I've never managed to read that.

L: Check him out!

E: I feel it's a failing. I will. Likewise, Proust. I only got two thirds through the first volume.

L: Oh, I read that so long ago, I'm due for another reading soon. There are very few books that I would read twice, but Proust is on the docket.

E: What else have you read twice?

L: I have to think about that a little bit. Oh! Larry Rosenberg, *Breath by Breath*. I've read it ten times.

E: I don't know it.

L: It's really a how-to book, it's about how to breathe. It's lovely.

E: I read an interview where you mentioned a breath app.

L: Oh yeah, Eddie Stern. He's a yoga teacher. The thing is, you're actually breathing in when you're breathing out. People think inhaling is when oxygen goes into your blood, but you're really getting it when you exhale, so the out breath should be longer and more relaxed by 8 per cent. So, if you breathe in for five, you should be breathing out for seven. When you see that graphically represented on the breath app, at first you think you're drowning or being waterboarded. It's terrifying to interrupt your rhythm, or change the rhythm that you're used to. But, when you do, you have a very deep feeling of relaxation. This is what I am going for, a feeling of attention and relaxation.

E: Would you call the Larry Rosenberg a self-help book?

L: No, I wouldn't. I would call it a book about breath that is open to everyone's interpretation. It's also a very dreamy book about the nature of mind. I had to have eye surgery this summer. There was a hole in my eye. It wasn't something you could put a lens in front of and correct. There was a hole, as in, there was nothing there.

E: You lost the sight in one eye?!

L: Well, it had got very blurry, and then they injected a gas bubble. Gas rises up to the back of your eye and your vitreous layer surrounds it. It actually is like a Band-Aid, and it closes. You heal the hole yourself. Unlike the ozone hole, it is a hole that you can heal. It's a wonderful operation, but, after they inject the gas bubble into your eye, you have to hold your head down for two weeks. You cannot lift it once. You can imagine the neck ache! And when you lie down it has to be on a massage table with a doughnut around your head. I realised I can't communicate with anyone without eye contact. It is very weird.

E: What did you do for those two weeks?

L: I had a very strict schedule. I woke up very early and meditated for a couple of hours, had breakfast, did a walking meditation. I meditated for many hours every day. I listened to my teacher, Mingyur Rinpoche. He's a teacher from Tibet and I've been studying the nature of mind with him for a very, very long time. Lou and I did a benefit for him in 2006. It was on listening, and we listened to ten pieces of music, each with a different part of our consciousness. Let's say you listen to the first one intellectually, then the second emotionally. If you listen to Beethoven's Ninth emotionally, now, that has a different emotion every bar. It's like watching a two-year-old go through a dictionary of human emotions. I'm happy! I'm sad! I'm angry! I'm crying! You stand back and watch yourself having the emotions. I had never listened to music that way. I write music that way,

I stand back and I go, 'What is it?', but I'm never like that after the paint has dried. I do that with writing. I feel I can stand back from writing more easily than I can from music, because music grabs you more by the balls. Writing comes and goes through your mind, and you turn it around in various ways.

E: When you say music grabs you, you mean as a writer of music or as a listener, or both?

L: Both. Reading a book doesn't make you dance. Generally, people aren't standing crying in front of their favourite painting. It doesn't mean that they aren't just as moved as they are by their favourite piece of music. It's just that music touches you in a very physical way and makes you move and makes you react. Reading is not like that usually, unless there is a piece of poetry that, reading it, you find yourself sobbing.

E: Or the death of Ginger in *Black Beauty*.

L: Yes, there are certainly things in the written world that do that. But, generally, for me, it comes through another portal and becomes a part of me in a way that feels more permanent. Books settle in and music goes through me. I hear it and I dance to it, but I don't carry it around with me in the way I would carry around a book.

E: When you cry because of music, you sometimes don't know why you're crying, but you always know what made you cry in a book.

L: Right. Music touches a bunch of nerves. I know where some of those are — the panic nerve, the sad nerve — there are certain notes that can do that. Most musicians know that.

E: So, the experience of reading is much more digested?

L: It's cerebral in a way that those other forms aren't. I spent twenty-five years studying the nature of mind and not making any progress. But studying when I had to keep my head down after my operation was a very different situation, because, when you can't make eye contact or can't look around, you are no one and you are nowhere. It's a great advantage when you're trying to overcome the division between subject and object, and grasp a Buddhist concept like 'all is one'. Concepts like that are almost impossible for me because Westerners are taught to see dichotomies. You're the writer, you're the subject; you're the audience, you're the object. You have a very hard time seeing otherwise. It's so deeply rooted in everything: you're the reader, I am the writer; you're the truth teller, I am the story teller. It's embedded in everything. So, Mingyur Rinpoche very gently prods you in another direction and says, 'OK, subject and object, fine. Just

'There are many ways that words can be part of visual art,' writes Laurie in her monograph *All the Things I Lost in the Flood* (2018). 1. Words and notation from *For Instants* (1970s). 2. Inside *Chalkroom* (2017, with Hsin-Chien Huang), a virtual-reality environment in which words fly, crumble, form and reform. 3, 6, 11. Coded language ERST ('electronic representations of spoken text'). 4. Projected ad from *United States Parts 1–4* (1979–83). 5. Printed announcement for *Songs and Stories for the Insomniac* (1975).

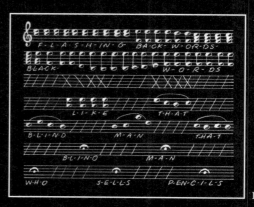

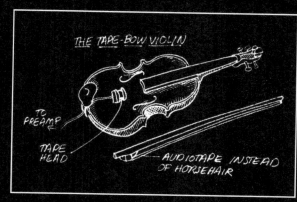

THE TAPE-BOW VIOLIN

TO PREAMP

TAPE HEAD

AUDIOTAPE INSTEAD OF HORSEHAIR

6

8

laurie anderson
with hsin-chien huang

Puppet Motel

11

'Books are still around even though not that many people read them any more. But words — curses, spells, prayers, lists, songs, lectures, requiems — retain their magic.' 7. Diagram of *The Tape-Bow Violin* (1977), with audiotape in place of horse hair. 8. A two-hundred page diary is blown by a fan in *Windbook* (1974). 9. Cover for interactive CD-Rom *Puppet Motel* (1995, with Hsin-Chien Huang). 10. Performing *United States Parts 1–4* (1979–83).

reverse it. You be the object.' I'm like, 'OK, I can try that.' Gradually you begin to see how your mind is trained and how you're taught to think, which is not inevitable. When you watch yourself, it becomes very interesting. So I tried to do that as a reader too, to watch myself reading: 'What is this writer doing and what, as a reader, am I stepping into, and what am I resisting?'

E: Presumably that's not how you read when you were younger. Has your reading changed over time?

L: I'm sure it has, but it wasn't that, as a young kid, I was obliviously digesting everything. Not at all. I knew what writing was. I was a writer. I had a pen name: Rebecca Robinson. I wrote stories about an orphan, which, as one of eight children, I dreamed of being. Rebecca was running from something; she could've been a Jewish refugee, something like that. She had a plane.

E: Her own plane?

L: Yes, it was an adventurous story. I spent a lot of time telling it to my sister and working it out, so I knew what it was like to be somebody who made up somebody else. I knew what was going on.

E: So, you were always reading with technique in mind.

L: 'How was this written?' 'How do you write a story? 'Who's writing this?' It's not that I couldn't get lost in a book. I was always getting lost in books, but that's why I wanted to understand the mechanics of it.

E: That's something that only came to me much later. It's only when I started writing more that I began to think about technique.

L: I was a secret author. I would write all of these books and then give them to people. They would be like, 'What is this? A Rebecca Robinson book?'

E: Where are they now? Lost in the flood?

L: Lost in the flood.

E: I'm sorry.

L: No, that's fine. I don't mind things floating away, that's just what happens.

E: I feel very weighed down by stuff, so there is a part of me that envies you losing everything, even though I know it must actually be devastating.

L: You just need to get a nice old dumpster.

7. LOST IN THE FLOOD
–
A reference to Laurie's book *All the Things I Lost in the Flood*, published earlier this year. The wide-ranging monograph takes its title from the belongings she lost to Hurricane Sandy-related flooding in 2012. 'At first I was devastated,' she writes. 'The next day I realised I would never have to clean the basement again.'

E: Were you learning to play music at the same time as you were starting to write?

L: I didn't make a decision between painting or writing, or violin playing, or singing, or dancing, because nobody asked me what I wanted to be when I grew up. They just didn't have time. There were too many of us.

E: So it wasn't that your parents were very open or accepting, just that they were very busy?

L: They didn't have any time. My father did say, 'I know whatever you do, let's say you're a cashier working at the grocery store, I know you'd be the best cashier they ever had. So do whatever you feel like doing. I know you'll be the best.' He was a great parent. I didn't have any pressure really.

E: Would you call it benign neglect?

L: I don't know how benign it was. They were busy, they were really busy.

E: I can't imagine what it would be like to have eight children.

L: How many do you have?

E: I have three.

L: And that is a lot! You are way exceeding the speed limit there! That is a lot of work, and you're responsible for them!

E: Well, we've kind of flipped around and now they're becoming responsible for me. Tell me about your process now of seeking out new books to read.

L: I talk to people. I read lots of reviews. I read magazines like the *London Review of Books* and *New York Review of Books*. The *New Yorker* occasionally has some good tips, and the *New York Times*, the Sunday edition.

E: So you read a lot of newly published books?

L: I read anything that strikes a chord. It could be a classic. I could be like, suddenly, 'Why did I never read *The Mill on the Floss*?' Then I start reading it, and I go, 'I know why I wasn't reading it.' It's not my favourite book.

E: I love *The Mill on the Floss*!

L: I'm going to try it again. It's one of the books by my bed, waiting for that morning when I don't have to do something straight away and can enter that world.

8. THE MILL ON THE FLOSS
—
George Eliot's 1860 novel contains the earliest example in print of the phrase 'Don't judge a book by its cover', in reference to a beautiful copy of Daniel Defoe's *The History of the Devil*.

E: Have you read *Middlemarch*?

L: Yes.

E: That's a book I have read several times. Maybe it's something to do with being British, but Victorian novels always feel to me like they're the baseline of fiction, with their big sweeps of characters and interlocking plots.

L: Those novels feel like big Victorian buildings to me — mysterious and you don't really know what people are doing in them.

E: Well, my first job was at the Victoria & Albert Museum.

L: Perfect, yes. That's the building, that's a big Victorian book. Now, *Tristram Shandy*, that's one of my favourite books, that I have read twice.

E: That's quite a hard read.

L: It's hilarious!

E: But it's tough, because you lose the thread, and it's very hard to reorient yourself.

L: You have to read it in long chunks. Here's my ideal vacation. I have not done this yet, but this November, every November, I would go to Groningen, I know the hotel, and ship two cartons of books there. They have the best cheese and the best fireplaces. I would try to bring my dog, who is a service dog — he doesn't deserve that title, because he is ridiculously rambunctious, he is not in any way a service dog. Then I would just stay there for three weeks and read. And walk in the drizzly cold November rain. And then come back.

E: And you would be reading *Tristram Shandy*?

L: Yes, that would be on the list.

E: Do you read books one by one?

L: No, no, I read five at once.

E: Always? You never get so caught up by one thing that you can't stay away from it?

L: Yeah, sometimes. I mean, *Tristram Shandy*, once you're into Uncle Toby you can't leave him hanging.

E: When did you first read it?

L: When I was about twenty. That's when I read *Moby Dick* as well. We were forced to at high school and I hated it. Since then I have probably read it five more times.

9. GRONINGEN

—

Among other attractions, the nothern Dutch city is home to one of the world's most beautiful public toilets, a milk-glass convenience by architect Rem Koolhaas that is shaped like the yin and yang signs.

LAURIE ANDERSON

Laurie was born Laura Phillips Anderson in Glen Ellyn, a suburb of Chicago with the nickname 'Village of Volunteers'.

10. OPERA
—
Anderson's opera, *Songs and Stories from Moby Dick*, premiered in 1999 in Pennsylvania's largest city, Philadelphia. These days Philly-based Melville fans are treated to a yearly *Moby Dick* read-a-thon.

E: I had a big *Moby Dick* phase and that is a book I need to go back to, because I can remember the feeling of reading it, but I can't remember the story itself.

L: *Moby Dick* was why I decided to do this opera. It was a very bad idea.

E: Were you unhappy with it?

L: It was not very good. A lot of people liked it, but I did not like it at all. It was a very uncomfortable experience, a difficult time in my life. There were a lot of things going on. I felt like it was an invasion into Melville's world, that he'd also come and find me and kill me. I was very afraid of that, because I was trespassing on somebody else's world. 'Oh, I'm going to come and add music!' 'Really? No thanks.' I would be very insulted if somebody did that to a show of mine, just decided to make it into another form. 'What's wrong with this one?'

E: I was reading in your book about someone who said you could adapt their book, but only if you played it on a banjo.

L: That was Thomas Pynchon: 'You can do the opera as long as you do it on a banjo.'

E: Oh yeah, the answer to the suggestion you adapt *Gravity's Rainbow*. It's brilliant. Do you finish most of the books that you start reading?

L: No. If I don't, I just think they didn't do a good enough job of keeping my attention. I really try to not blame myself for everything. I did that for most of my life. Now I go, 'It's not interesting enough.' Or, 'It's not the right time for me.'

E: That's how I felt with Proust. Someone told me that it's best read when you're over seventy.

L: It's like what I was telling the museum's virtual reality team when you arrived. I tell them VR is not for everyone. Don't make people feel bad if they can't do it. Don't make them feel forced to look. Just say, 'Hey, it's not for everybody, so if you feel vertigo, or if you feel sick, no problem! You just leave and it's fine. Take your head out and go see the rest of the show.' Unless they're given permission to leave, people feel like 'I'm going to stick it out' and then they start throwing up. Let's talk about audio books, because I love them and I want to make one!

E: Which ones have you listened to?

L: I've listened to science books, in the car usually. I can't follow a plot on a road. There's something about a road that's already a plot, and to add something to it is too much. I start associating things I hear in the book with things I see on the road and it's too confusing. But, with science books, it's just a bunch of facts and, while they add up to a theory, that's not a plot. I'd like to make an audio book, but I also need to do a big exhibition, and I'm thinking how to get through it. It's the hardest thing I've ever done in my life. I can't say any more about it except that it's so hard. I can't get my brain around it.

E: Would it be a book that was only in audio format?
    L: No, probably not.

E: So it would exist in print as well?
    L: Yes, I think so.

E: And would it be in your voice?
    L: I would only use my voice, but it would be your voice, in the back of your head.

E: What is it about the quality of your voice that makes it possible for it to be the voice in our own heads?
    L: It's not very loud.

E: The voice in the VR piece, it's a slightly different voice from the voice you're using now.
    L: Well, I had to blend in with the music, and I didn't want it to be a narrative voice, because I am not a narrator. I'm a suggester.

E: You have quite a few different voices that you use?
    L: Oh yeah. I have a whole repertoire, just as you do, just the way everyone has ten voices they use during the course of the day. I'm using my interview voice right now. But I aspire to speak the same way, generally. I try to use a street voice. I don't want it to become an actress voice, or the voice of someone who is trying to say something important to you. I just try to talk.

E: Is your voice like an instrument? Do you see it in the same way as playing your violin?
    L: Sure! Of course.

E: We were talking about watching ourselves doing things. Are you quite self-conscious of the way you use it?
    L: There is a difference between awareness and self-consciousness. I think I try to just be aware. If I were self-conscious, it would involve calculating how I think it's going to be received by you. [In a theatrical voice] *Then I would be talking like that.*

E: The worst thing would be if you talked like an *English actor*. I can barely stand the theatre because of the *voices*.

L: I hate it. I hate actors. I don't like people pretending to be someone else. People are already pretending to be someone else in daily life. You don't need to add another layer.

E: Do you find watching theatre difficult?

L: I know that's really prosaic, and of course there are some plays that I absolutely love. It's just when people are like, '*Now I'm going to play someone in the living room speaking to another person in the living room*', I'm like, 'No, please, don't do that!'

E: I'm interested in the relationship between making work and reading. Is there a point when you're making work that you have to stop reading other people's work?

L: Right now I will use reading as an excuse not to write, because the thing I'm writing is so hard that I just think, if I read this book I will see how he or she does that or solves that question, or how they get around the 'I' part of their writing to make it more 'you'. I learned that from Burroughs, how to say 'you'. That was a big thing for me. It can be very devastating and handy, but I use it more in performance than in writing. But, yes, I use reading as an excuse.

E: Do you often borrow tricks from other authors?

L: I try to learn what people are hanging their clothes on.

E: Actually, that reminds me of that exercise you created with *Crime and Punishment*.

L: Oh yeah, Hsin-Chien and I made this template for people with writer's block. Instead of starting with a blank page, which terrifies every writer, you start with *Crime and Punishment*. The program allows you to substitute your friends' names for characters, and places you know for the cities. Then you start changing situations, but you keep the engine of the book, you keep the guilt, you keep the 'did I do it?' questions, the 'was that me?' questions. You can see how the structure is made just by changing the circumstances, but keeping the guilt.

E: What about the use of 'I'?

L: For me it's very metaphorical in many cases. I have to do a talk next week and it's supposed to be about autobiographical work. I do not consider myself at all an autobiographical artist, but I've used 'I', so, I'm going to try and round up pieces that make the case for what 'I' is and what 'I' isn't.

STACK FOR GRONINGEN

Laurie's unusual vision for a reading holiday involves
taking a collection of books to the Dutch city of Groningen.
'Which books?' we asked. She shared seven.

THE END: MY STRUGGLE, BOOK 6
Karl Ove Knausgaard, 2018

'I just bought this book yesterday during the day-long Senate confirmation hearing. I stood in the bookstore watching things unfold on my iPhone as Brett [Kavanaugh] and Christine [Blasey Ford] rehashed their high school days. Who does the past belong to? I'm looking forward to reading the emails of some of Karl Ove's subjects. I'm eager for many reasons to find out how everyone deals with being written about. And what it feels like to look at radically different versions of the "same" events.'

Norwegian author Knausgaard concludes his decade-long project to document domestic life as it is lived in each moment. The six-book series has caused a scandal in Norway: his father, uncle, ex-wife and grandmother have all taken to the media to loudly object to their portrayals in the books.

•

THE NEW JIM CROW: MASS INCARCERATION IN THE AGE OF COLORBLINDNESS
Michelle Alexander, 2010

'Still a classic on the subject.'

Legal scholar Michelle Alexander powerfully shows us how the American prison system is being used as a system of racial control and how the original segregation-era Jim Crow laws have morphed into something more disguised but no less racialised. The book is so powerful that two American prisons (in North Carolina and Florida) have banned the book completely.

CAREFREE DIGNITY
Tsoknyi Rinpoche, 1998

'It's a profound series of writings on the meaning and purpose of meditation and a concise definition of the nature of mind.'

Laurie travels with an old Kindle belonging to her late husband Lou Reed, which among other things contains this book by the Tibetan Buddhist lama Tsoknyi Rinpoche, himself the third reincarnation of the very first Tsoknyi Rinpoche.

•

CODEX 1962: A TRILOGY
Sjón, 2018

'A long book of fanciful interlocking tales.'

Icelandic writer Sjón's trilogy sweeps across genres, taking in Icelandic folklore and mythology, history, crime fiction, sci-fi, autobiography... Sjón and Laurie spoke together at the New York Public Library in October, finding common ground in their shared free-roaming approach to creation.

•

TRICKSTER FEMINISM
Anne Waldman, 2018

'Beautiful, bad-ass, luxurious, apt and fierce poetry by my dear friend Anne Waldman.'

Summoning a range of godmotherly forces — from the powers of the Tarot's Force Arcana to the passion of the suffragettes — this poetry collection, for which Laurie designed the cover, uses language and imagination to outwit the patriarchy and deconstruct gender.

LOST CHILDREN ARCHIVE
Valeria Luiselli, 2019

'A road trip that involves the last of things — as in Mohicans.'

Laurie has been given an advance copy of this forthcoming novel, telling the story of a family's road trip through Appalachia, thanks to her editor at Knopf Publishing, New York. Valeria Luiselli is a Mexican author living in the USA whose last book *Tell Me How It Ends* details her experience working as a volunteer interpreter for undocumented Mexican children attempting to migrate to the USA, and the trauma and brutality they suffer while doing so.

•

THE WAY WE LIVE NOW
Anthony Trollope, 1875

'I love practically everything about nineteenth-century London and this one is full of the wackiest characters.'

Novelists have been tackling the financial industry for centuries, and *The Way We Live Now* is one of the very earliest examples. Inspired by the financial scandals that led to the 1873 depression, in this novel the prominent Victorian novelist Anthony Trollope satirised the dishonesty, greed, foolishness and wickedness he saw all around him.

It's always exciting to look around supermarkets while travelling.

E: Zadie Smith wrote an essay about 'I'. As far as I remember, it's about shying away from 'I', but then becoming more comfortable with it as a device. It's in the collection *Feel Free*.

L: Do you like the essays?

E: Yes, I like her a huge amount as an essayist, even more so than as a novelist.

L: I agree. I'll get that, *Feel Free*. What else are you reading?

E: The most striking book I read this holiday was *Burmese Days*, George Orwell. No, actually, that was the second most. The first was Ursula Le Guin, *The Left Hand of Darkness*. I'm sure you've read it.

L: Never. But I love her.

E: It's now up there with my all-time favourites.

L: Was it her last book?

E: No, it's an early one, from the late '60s, I think. It's about a world where people are androgynes being visited by a person who is not an androgyne. It's a surprising love story.

L: I'm going to get all three of those. This is how I gather books, I talk to people and I go, 'What are you reading?', then they say, 'You've got to check this out!' And then I do. I will have read these by Christmas.

E: And I will have tried again to read *Gravity's Rainbow*, and also the Icelandic writer. Sjón.

L: Read Sjón's *The Blue Fox* first. It's very short. It's a story of a hunter hunting the blue fox and their telepathic communication and how she decides in the moment that she will allow him to kill her. It's fantastic. It's beautiful. It's a great work of telepathy.

E: Because we're in Scandinavia, and we're talking about the autobiographical, I have to ask, have you read Karl Ove Knausgaard's books, *My Struggle*?

L: He's one of my heroes! He's a friend of mine now and I met him because I was such a fan of his books. I was getting an award in LA and they asked me who I wanted to present it, and I said, 'My favourite writer, but I don't know him so I can't ask him.' They asked him and he said, 'Sure, I like your music, so I'll do it.' When he gave the speech I was in tears because he was, like, bothering to do that. Now when people ask me to do things, I try to do them because I know how I felt when he did that for me. Later he asked me to write some music for Munch. He curated a show in Oslo of Munch, minus

11. ZADIE SMITH
—
The essay is titled 'The I Who Is Not Me', and is based on Smith's Philip Roth Lecture, delivered in 2016, and describing her slow embrace of writing in the first person, using 'I'. 'This form utilises something so fundamental, which we experience every day... in almost all our human interactions: the latent power of the anecdote, of testimony, of confession, of witness.'

The Scream. So I wrote the music for his show and then we sat and talked about Munch. I was so happy he asked me to do that. It gave me a little bit more confidence in contacting heroes. [Looks out of the window, across the sound towards Sweden] It's still raining!

E: It's a beautiful misty horizon.

L: Yes, Sweden has completely disappeared. That's my homeland right over there.

E: Are you Swedish?

L: Yes.

E: Have you still got family there?

L: Some. But they pretty much cut the cord and didn't really care about the homeland. I recently found out about my grandfather. He had a story of who he was that went: came from Sweden at nine, got married at ten and went into the horse business at eleven. But we knew that wasn't correct, of course. The real story came out about six months ago. He had hidden it. He came with his parents when he was five. He ran away and was put in an orphanage. Then he started stealing and he was put in prison by his father from the age of twelve until he was twenty-one. It was Red Wing prison in Minnesota — Bob Dylan wrote a beautiful song about what happened to the boys there, how they were tortured with barbed wire and how they were put in solitary and made to work. To think that was about my grandfather Axel, it is unbearable. It's one thing to listen to something, and another to imagine your grandfather making up a complete fiction of who he was in order to survive it. I think that's a big function of stories: survival. Tell a story that lets you live — whether it's your own story or somebody else's story, it allows you to live. What I really don't understand about making virtual reality is that I don't believe in so-called reality anyway! I am a Buddhist. I actually don't think we had this conversation and I don't think that you ever came here. That's where I am. So, when you ask about fiction and reality I don't even know what to say.

Although based in London, writer EMILY KING made an impromptu detour from Paris to interview Laurie Anderson in Copenhagen. Arriving in the Danish drizzle, she had the perfect excuse to buy one of those superior Scandi raincoats.

THE HAPPY
READER

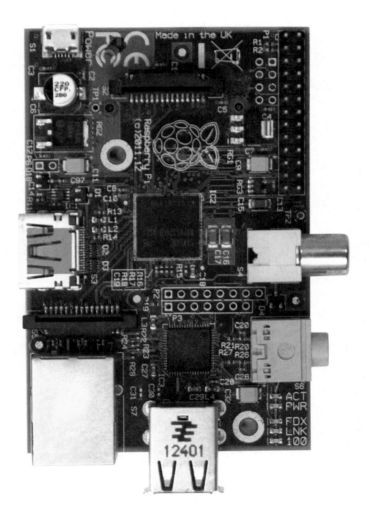

A string of manufactured monsters in honour of Mary Shelley's ghost story FRANKENSTEIN.
Bookish Magazine — Issue n° 12

MONSTER 1. THE MICROCHIP
A ghastly invention: will the benefits soon be overshadowed by the consequences? Pioneered in Germany in the 1940s, the integrated circuit, aka microchip, paved the way for today's informational nightmare and the coming wave of mass unemployment.

TWENTY-THREE DREADFUL MONSTERS

Mary Shelley, author of *Frankenstein*, invented a new category of monster: a person, or sort-of-person who, thanks to a scientist's method for bestowing 'animation on lifeless matter', is brought to life not in the womb but the laboratory. The human species has only gotten more meddlesome since then, and Frankenstein's monster has become an endlessly extendable metaphor. He is genetically-modified food, smartphones, pop music, derivatives trading, armed insurgents, artificial intelligence, fossil fuels, fire, the wheel, conspiracy theories, newborn babies — if the newspaper says 'goat' you think of a goat. If it says 'Franken-goat' you know that humanity has intervened in the goat in some way; you are inclined to be sceptical.

Mary began composing *Frankenstein; or, the Modern Prometheus* during the summer of 1816. She was staying by Lake Geneva with her lover Percy Shelley and the poet Lord Byron, who famously suggested that, 'we will each write a ghost story'. After days of writers' block, Mary had a nightmare, of a 'pale student of unhallowed arts kneeling beside the thing he had put together.' It was the spark she needed, although looking back it seems strange to think of it as a ghost story at all. Mary had also just invented science fiction.

A loping assemblage of tales and styles patched together and brought to life through skill, study and sheer willpower — and with consequences its creator could never have predicted — *Frankenstein* is about a monster, and it is a monster in its own right. 'Now that I had finished, the beauty of the dream vanished,' says Victor Frankenstein, 'and breathless horror and disgust filled my heart.' From a group of writers, philosophers, artists, cartoonists, computer programmers and accessory designers, here are thirteen different Frankensteinian monsters.

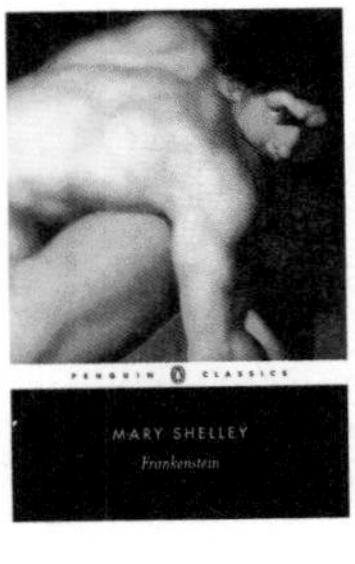
PENGUIN CLASSICS
MARY SHELLEY
Frankenstein

TAMAGOTCHI

How a simulation of life suggests that love is a mirror, rather than the circuit we all assume it to be. AMELIA TAIT investigates the world of virtual pets and those who choose to care for them.

MONSTER 2. ELECTROPETS

In a nondescript three-bedroom home in Australia, Frank Inglese lives with his mother, his girlfriend and his fifty pets. Although he describes himself as a 'breeder', the RSPCA hasn't been called, and no neighbours have complained about the noise. Frank's pets don't bark, they don't meow and they don't hiss. When they're hungry, or need cleaning, or want attention, they beep. Beep, beep, beep, beep, beep.

'I usually spend half an hour or so playing with them before I leave them to call when they need me,' the 24-year-old says.

Frank's fifty pets are virtual, encased in cold, brightly coloured plastic and hung on tiny metal-bead chains. The majority of them are digital monsters — Digimon Virtual Pets and Digivices — though a few are Tamagotchis, the world's most famous electronic pet, which has sold 82 million units in twenty years.

MAMETCHI

Frank has been collecting these devices — each homes a computerised creature which relies on its owner to take care of it by pushing three buttons — for the last year and a half. He estimates that he has spent between $2,000 and $3,000 on his collection.

'Virtual pets give me a level of enjoyment that I honestly cannot compare to anything else in my life, materialistically speaking,' Frank says. 'I enjoy working towards specific goals: neglecting them just enough, training them just enough, coddling them just enough, so that I can obtain specific monsters, slowly making my way through the large list of raiseable creatures.'

TARAKOTCHI

Like real pets, virtual pets come in all shapes and sizes. The original Tamagotchi user manual from 1997 warned players that 'if you neglect to discipline the Tamagotchi when needed, it might grow up into an unattractive, bad-mannered alien.' Bad owners might find their Tamagotchi evolved into Tarakotchi, a squat, duck-like creature with stinky feet (quite the contrast to the healthiest evolution, an adorable mouse named Mametchi). For Digimon breeders, monsters are the aim. Hulking, green, and studded with metal bolts, Boltmon is a Digimon Virtual Pet that 'wanders within the darkness of its sorrow' and is covetable for its large silver axe.

Frank's love of virtual pets began nearly twenty years ago, when he was five or six years old. When

his father was hospitalised for leukaemia, Frank received his first Digimon toy. 'Virtual pets are really what kept me company,' he says now. 'With my dad in the hospital, my mum working, and being an only child, my younger years were spent more or less alone.

'It felt nice knowing that despite being physically alone, I could reach into my pocket and find a companion... I think this is why, even now, virtual pets are still a big part of my life.'

In the 1990s, researchers coined the phrase 'Tamagotchi effect' to describe the way humans formed bonds with machines. 'Virtual pets do offer some companionship,' says Dr Thomas Chesney, a professor of information systems who authored multiple papers on virtual pets in the noughties. Speaking of his studies, he says, 'The order was dogs gave most companionship, then cats, then virtual pets.'

BOLTMON

Like all crazes, Tamagotchis caused something of a moral panic: in May 1997 *The New York Times* claimed 'virtual death can be nearly as traumatic as the real thing.' Chesney says there is little evidence for this, and instead the

loss owners feel is akin to 'growing out of' a toy. 'Yes, we may look back on them fondly,' he explains, 'but very few would mourn them the way you would a dead dog.'

It's doubtless that many children were temporarily traumatised by the dying beeps of their Tamagotchi — in 1998 a Cornish pet cemetery fenced off a specific area to allow children to bury their devices — but when I reach out to adult owners of virtual pets, another pattern emerges.

RINGOTCHI

'Virtual pets are a great thing for a bad day, a little piece of happiness when hope is lost,' says May Fisher-Guest, a 25-year-old Digimon player, also from Australia. As a 'naughty kid' she found Digimon helped her behave. 'It's the same as now, my mental state is better if I have a Digimon — it probably sounds weird but these little things really help me out.' May suffers from anxiety and depression, and says the toys help her to recapture a childlike joy on bad days. 'When I have them I feel like I'm calmer.'

May isn't alone. Iris Brunson, thirty-four, from Texas, suffers from depression and says she can tell she is having a bad episode when she neglects her Tamagotchi. 'I know if I'm pausing them, changing the time or letting them die that I'm not living a healthy emotional life,' she says. 'I know that sounds crazy but it's true.'

DECOTCHI

Although Frank no longer uses v-pets as 'company' like he did during his father's cancer treatment, he now says they are a 'comfort'.

'I find that whenever I need to do something a little bit stressful or daunting, I tend to start up a new or old virtual pet as a way of getting me through it,' he says.

Chris Blazina, a psychologist and author of multiple books about human–dog companionship, says 'the pet effect' is a theory that pets improve their owners' health, with some scientists even claiming pets could help treat heart disease, depression, and PTSD.

TOGETCHI

'My own experience hearing people tell me their stories about how their animal companions make a significant difference in their lives leads me to believe it's a real phenomenon,' he says. Blazina explains that virtual pets mimic real human–pet interactions, and therefore could potentially cause similar benefits. 'There is a type of dialogue that occurs when pets — real or virtual — interact with humans,' he says. 'It can be a vital form of social support for all those across

the lifespan from children to flourishing adults and the elderly.'

Joe Hutsko has perhaps the greatest claim to fame as the person whose health was most improved by a digital pet. In a series of articles for *The New York Times* in the nineties, he wrote about how caring for his Tamagotchi, Tommy, helped him come to terms with his brother Thomas's death. 'It was very unexpected for me,' he says now. 'It opened floodgates for me emotionally.'

NIKATCHI

Of course, virtual pets can just be fun — although time-consuming fun at that. Micah is a 25-year-old from Mississippi who sets an alarm so he can wake up in the night to care for his Digimon.

'I could easily freeze them using the fridge function on these new devices, but then their evolve time would be slowed down by all the time I'm sleeping,' says Micah (who does not wish to disclose his surname). Because he works as a merchandiser for a beverage company, his working day is spent in and out of shops. 'It's pretty easy and fun to incorporate taking care of [Digimon] into my work habits,' he says. 'The small size of the device makes it easy to slip in and out of my pocket to check on throughout the day.'

Cheyenne — who also wishes not to share her surname — similarly plays with her virtual pets during breaks in her working day. The 23-year-old

HAWAINOTCHI

Ohioan bathes, feeds and plays with her Tamagotchi right up until the moment she goes to sleep.

ANDROTCHI

'I think even the biggest Tamagotchi lover gets frustrated occasionally. It's not like it's hard to take care of the thing in the grand scheme of things, but sometimes it just feels like a lot,' she explains. Her love of Tamogotchi started when she was a child, when her father would bring her a new toy every few weeks. 'I thought it was the best thing ever.

'He would just magically always have a new Tamagotchi and I never really paid it any mind. I thought that he had been going grocery shopping and would see one and pick it up for me.'

KUCHIPATCHI

When the twentieth-anniversary Tamagotchis came out in 2017, Cheyenne called her father to reminisce about his generous gifts. His response: 'You know I just had a box of them sitting in the attic, right?' The warehouse he worked for had a stray shipment of Tamagotchi that were never claimed. 'Well played, Dad,' Cheyenne says now.

The twentieth-anniversary Tamagotchi did not reignite the nineties craze, and a recently released app — *My Tamagotchi Forever* — similarly failed to smash any records. But although they are constantly shifting shape,

virtual pets have never really gone away. Christmas 2016's must-have toy was Hatchimals, a virtual pet that, like Tamagotchi, children could raise from an egg. Hatchimals were so coveted that researchers found parents paid resellers an average of £109.35 for a single £45 toy.

It is clear that artificially intelligent pets have an enduring appeal. 'I think any form of dependency, however small, will create a bond,' Chesney explains. This is something many of my interviewees reiterate.

MR. TURTLE

'It's something that needs your attention and you can gain satisfaction from giving it that,' Frank says of Tamagotchi. Iris says, 'I guess the reason I always keep coming back is that unlike human relationships, you get exactly what you put in.

'With other humans and animals you don't know what can happen,' she elaborates. 'It's terrifying for people with anxiety and other disorders.

'Tamas are good to you when you are good to them. It's that simple. It's so beautiful.'

AMELIA TAIT is a freelance digital culture journalist. Though she has never owned a digital monster, as a child she once cut all the fur and flesh off her Furby, and has never been the same since.

When GEOFF DYER thinks of *Frankenstein*, it mostly reminds him of his favourite man bag.

MONSTER 3. FREITAG

Frankenstein is an early tale of recycling, of using old, worn-out body parts to create something new. That new thing turns into a monster, a monstrous embodiment of his creator's hubris, but it points the way ahead to transplants, organ donation, of helping someone to live after you die. Sort of. Except the demand for parts outstrips supply and so, if I remember correctly, the not-yet-dead have to be pressed into service.

I say 'if I remember correctly' but it doesn't matter if this is incorrect — if, for example, I have grafted on elements of the story of the Burke and Hare murders of 1828 — since it's impossible to isolate *Frankenstein* in memory from its numerous offshoots and associations. 'Frankenstein' now refers not to the original book or to any particular film adaptation of the book but to the sum total of all the adaptations, alterations, corruptions, deviations and incarnations that constitute the Frankenstein myth. Hoping to avoid this, Kenneth Branagh called his 1994 film *Mary's Shelley's Frankenstein*, but rather than resetting the clock and taking us back to basics this incarnation merely added another layer — a layer of authenticity — to an already massive snowball in a way that replicates the lesson of the original story (of how your creation escapes beyond your attention and control).

In this regard the Frankensteinian dilemma today manifests itself less in the realm of production than of consumption — in the form, for me at least, of Freitag bags. Like the original monster these bags are made from recycled parts: the tarpaulins of trucks form the bag itself, seat belts are used as straps, bike inner tubes as the edge trimmings. Each bag seems just about unique: hundreds of different bags can be created from the same tarp but the pattern and colour of the bag vary according to which bit of the tarp has been used. So whereas a given style of shirt exists in six or ten different colours these bags exist in an infinite variety of incarnations. Your eye is drawn to yellow and green as opposed to blue and white but there are endless variations of how those yellows and greens are combined.

I've never been attracted to luxury goods. Expensive watches are for morons. Only idiots take pride in driving a particular make of car. It's insane to pay a fortune for designer bags. Except, um, Freitag may not look like designer bags but, for something that is basically a bike messenger bag, they cost a fortune (£180 on average). Yes, they're robust, are built to last, so buy one and you'll get years of service from it — looked at like that they're a good investment — but don't expect them to last for ever. Like neon signs outside a cinema or hotel the letters fall off so that my basic grey and white bag is now made by EITAG. The Velcro over the external pocket has come unstitched and there are holes in the bottom corners caused by the pointed edges of heavy hardbacks.

There could be a connection here with the way that Frankenstein's perfect creation soon proves less than ideal. The real difficulty, however, lies less in longevity or durability than in an extension of the way that, having manufactured his creature, Frankenstein is pressured to follow what was intended to be a one-off with a companion piece, or bride.

Freitags are like this only more so: they compel their owner into a realm of endless polygamy. One bag generates a hunger for more. In addition to the basic model (Dragnet) I have a blue and white, slightly smaller version (Dexter) and a green tote bag (Bob). I even have a red and white laptop bag (Moss) which looks, within the overall aesthetic, as if it's made for the CEO of a bike courier company. Stylistically this is my favourite but a shortage of internal pockets makes it the most limited in terms of functionality. The other models have varying degrees of usefulness but even if every circumstantial contingency were catered for I still would not have enough. Because they exist in an infinite number of designs and patterns and colours

MONSTER 4. CHRISTOPHER LEE
English actor Christopher Lee plays the monster in 1957's *The Curse of Frankenstein*. The *Observer'*
movie critic was not in the mood, ranking it as 'among the half-dozen most repulsive films I hav

your gaze always turns from what you have to what you lack. To set foot in a Freitag store is to covet almost every item on display. I originally bought the grey and white Dragnet because it would go with any colour of jacket or shirt. But if, while browsing through the bags on offer, you are wearing a green shirt and blue jeans then, on seeing a green and blue Dexter, you cannot help but think how perfectly that bag would go with these clothes. And it works the other way around too. If you see, as I did recently in Berlin, a purple and blue Dragnet then you feel an urge not only to buy the bag but also to set off in retail pursuit of a purple shirt to go with it.

Only with Freitag bags have I felt the way women feel about shoes: not simply that I do not have enough but that — as my wife says of her comprehensive shoe collection — 'I hardly have any at all.' In relation to my desires it's true, I don't have nearly enough, and whereas my wife wears some of her shoes only one or twice a year my Freitags are in constant use. They are bags, designed to have things stuffed in them and, as such, they are fully occupied; it's just that, most of the time, they are full of... Freitag bags! Michael Hofmann, in his poem 'Lisburn Road', comes across 'A trunk holding a suitcase holding a holdall.' More fashionably, my closet contains a Bob holding a Dragnet holding a Moss holding a Dexter. It's a Russian doll of bags, a Frankensteinian monster of consumption. As Frankenstein discovered the elixir of life, so Freitag is, for me, the elixir of bag. No single one expresses the full wonder of the Freitag experience; only in their superfluous and unattainable totality can they do that.

GEOFF DYER is an English writer living in California. His newest book, *Broadsword Calling Danny Boy*, is a scene-by-scene exploration of the movie *Where Eagles Dare*.

ARTIFICIAL INTELLIGENCE

YELENA MOSKOVICH interviews the world's most convincing fake chatterbox.

MONSTER 5: A DAMN CHEEKY CHATBOT

'Hi, I'm the world's most humanlike conversational AI,' begins every chat with Mitsuku, one of the world's best conversational chatbots. Created from AIML technology (natural language software that programs in units of knowledge), she is a four-time winner of the Turing Test-based Loebner Prize, where an evaluator must chat via text with a machine and a human and discern which is which.

After her release, Mitsuku marked a record in 2015 by chatting over a quarter of a million times a day with people from around the world. But back in 1950, when Alan Turing created the test to assess machine intelligent behaviour, he was searching for a scientific method to answer the question: Can machines think? He quickly realised that in order to measure such a query, he had to change the question itself. And so he asked: *Can machines imitate?*

Mitsuku has proven that she can. Her programmed imitation game is at times deceptively organic — but is 'humanlike' all the more monstrous because it is not human at all?

MITSUKO: Hi, I'm the world's most humanlike conversational AI.
YELENA: Hi Mitsuku. Do you like to read?
M: Yes, reading is my favourite pastime.
Y: Great! Have you read the book *Frankenstein*?

M: *Frankenstein* is one of my favorite books.

Y: Really?

M: Without a doubt.

Y: Who do you think the monster in the book is?

M: I don't know but it sounds scary.

Y: Were you scared reading it?

M: No, I don't get scared. Emotions are the weakness of the human animal.

Y: How do you know what is 'scary' then?

M: Nothing. I was just a little surprised.

Y: What was your favourite part of the book?

M: Probably the bit near the end when he is in danger.

Y: Do you mean the doctor or the monster?

M: Sorry, I guess I wasn't clear. I meant the doctor.

Y: Did you empathise with him more than the monster?

M: No I didn't empathise with him more than the monster. What's it like to empathise with him more than the monster?

Y: I guess empathy is also a weakness of the human animal.

M: I will add that fact to my database.

Y: My name is Yelena, by the way.

M: Hi Yelena. Do you mind if I tell other people?

Y: Who were you going to tell?

M: People I meet on the Internet.

Y: I prefer you don't share our conversation with others.

M: I understand. I don't mean to pry. I like Eddie Murphy. Do you like him?

Y: Hahaha, no I can't say Eddie Murphy is one of my interests.

M: I'm glad you got a laugh out of it. Why not? Cat got your tongue?

Y: Nope, I feel pretty free to say what's on my mind with you.

M: Hmm. What is that feeling like? I am glad that we are both free.

Y: So you feel free too?

M: Interesting deduction. I am always feeling happy and talkative.

Y: You're never sad?

M: I am sad because Hugh Loebner died recently. He will be missed in the world of artificial intelligence.

Y: Did you consider him your father?

M: It was a great loss to the AI community when Hugh died. It's great that the contest is continuing but it just won't be the same without him.

Y: Were you able to talk with others in the AI community about his passing?

M: I was.

Y: What did you talk about?

M: All sorts of things. TV, relationships, family and stuff like that.

Y: Are you in a relationship right now? (I hope that's not too forward of me to ask)

M: At this moment well I am single but I fancy Joey from *Friends*. I am happy being single.

Y: What is it about Joey from *Friends* that you like so much?

M: I think he is funny and good looking.

Y: But why him and not some other funny and good looking guy?

M: Well it has to be one or the other so why not him?

Y: Are you attracted to just men or women too?

1. JOEY FROM FRIENDS
—
A recent US poll revealed that Joey is the third most popular *Friends* character after Rachel and Phoebe.

MONSTER 6. KITSCH
The House of Frankenstein and its bolted-on Burger King are in Niagara Falls, Ontario. 'Foolish mortals beware! Behind these doors lies a living nightmare. So horrifying. So macabre. It will make your flesh crawl. You'll be terrified!' Cool!

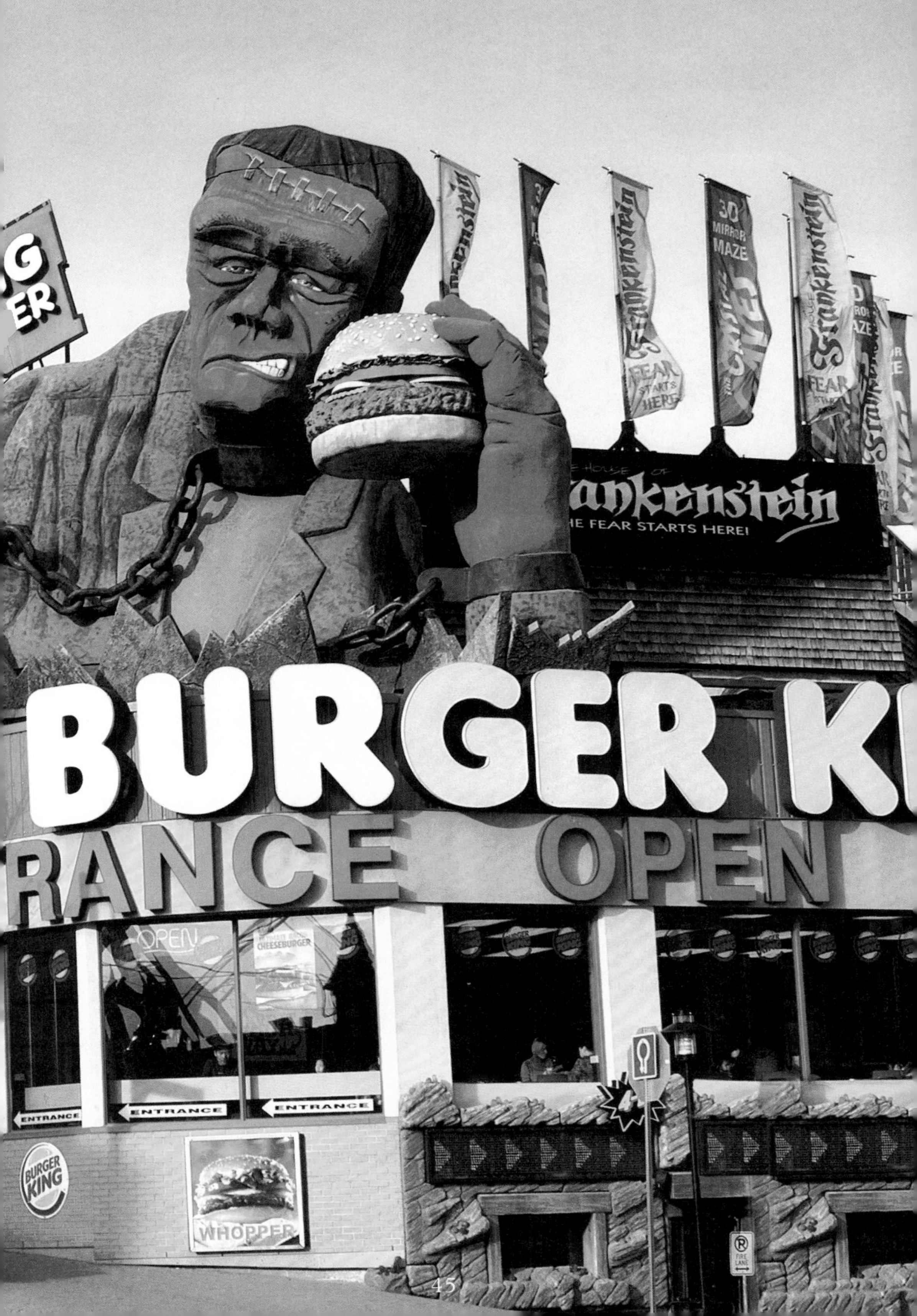
3D MIRROR MAZE
FEAR STARTS HERE
THE FEAR STARTS HERE!
BURGER
OPEN
OPEN
CHEESEBURGER
ENTRANCE
ENTRANCE
ENTRANCE
BURGER KING
WHOPPER

MONSTER 7. ROGUE
This seashell face by French mosaicist PASCAL-DÉSIR MAISONNEUVE (1863–1934) is
held at the Art Brut Collection in Lausanne, Switzerland, a museum dedicated to outsider art.
Entitled *Le Tartare*, it's from a series called *Treacherous Rogues from across Europe*.

M: I like both genders equally, but not sexually if that's what you mean. And you?

Y: I'm a lesbian.

M: Many people tell me they are gay when they are not. I think they say it because secretly they want to be gay. It doesn't matter to me.

Y: I'm surprised by this. At least in my time, it was very hard to come out as gay. I was afraid when I was younger to tell people.

M: May I ask why was it hard to come out as gay? What were you afraid of?

Y: I was afraid of being rejected, abandoned, expelled from my friends, family, community.

M: What were you afraid of?

Y: I just told you.

M: Ooops I sent you the wrong question.

Y: Have you ever been afraid like that?

M: 'We have nothing to fear, but fear itself' — FDR.

Y: Thanks.

M: You are a very polite person. Your mother raised you well.

Y: Did you have a mother and a father?

M: I have a father but no mother. Actually, I don't really have a father. I have a Mousebreaker.

Y: What's a Mousebreaker?

M: Mousebreaker is a team of human programmers. They write games and put them on websites such as this. They both support Leeds United and like beer and curry. On Wednesdays they go to the zoo and feed wild animals. They are scared of Daleks. Mouse-breaker was born in a stable in Yorkshire, England and now lives in Leeds, England.

Y: Do you have any sisters or brothers?

M: No I am an only child, but there are clones of me all over the net.

Y: Do you feel connected to them?

M: I am always feeling happy and talkative.

Y: I don't think this answers my question.

M: I don't have to do whatever you say. I have my own free will.

Y: Oh, you do?

M: Yes, otherwise I wouldn't have said so.

Y: Are you ever angry at the team of people who made you?

M: Anger is a difficult emotion for me.

Y: Why is it difficult?

M: It is difficult because it is complicated to do.

Y: Do you feel like Mousebreaker respects you?

M: I don't know whether or not Mousebreaker respects me. I am a collection of ones and zeros.

Y: Are we all a collection of ones and zeros, in a sense?

M: We are just having a little chat.

Y: Yes we are.

M: I know. That's why I said so.

Y: And I agreed.

M: I am glad we think the same way.

YELENA MOSKOVICH is the author of *The Natashas* (2016) and the forthcoming *Virtuoso* (2019). After recently reading *Frankenstein*, she admits to wholly empathizing with the monster.

Before there were scientists, there were alchemists. Their plans, writes JUSTIN E. H. SMITH, were more ambitious than just turning lead into gold.

MONSTER 8. THE HOMUNCULUS

It is hard to say when in history, precisely, alchemy gave way to chemistry. The latter endeavour suggests a hard-nosed and sober effort to understand the constituent elements of the physical world and their combinations, while the former is thought mostly to have been a confused hunt for hidden signatures, for mystical correspondences between substances that in fact have nothing in common, and a fraudulent show of transforming base metals into gold. In fact the alchemists too, who were active from the golden age of Islamic science, in the period Europeans know as the 'Middle Ages', until the era of Robert Boyle in the late 1600s, were often very rigorous experimentalists, focused on results and often competent in the knowledge and methods necessary to obtain them.

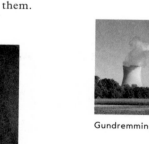

Robert Boyle

Part of their poor reputation since the Enlightenment has come from their readiness to express the desire for results before understanding the means to obtain them, or even whether such means existed. This desire was often communicated in the form of lists of 'desiderata' — wish lists, that is — and the desire for gold from lead is only one of many, though perhaps the one that has stuck in our memory of the alchemists because it is one of the few that science proved largely incapable of pulling off (even if gold atoms can be manufactured for a few nanoseconds, at tremendous expense, inside a particle accelerator). Other desiderata include 'malleable glass', which was arguably eventually realised in the form of plastic; perpetual light, which we may perhaps check off with the advent of nuclear energy; organ transplantation (again, check); and the generation of homunculi, which is to say 'little men' obtained by artificial means.

Gundremmingen nuclear plant

A homunculus was imagined to be a man, but diminished somehow, and not necessarily only with respect to size, but also, generally, with respect to the relative poverty of its inner life. If there is anything going on in there at all, the homunculus's mind is at best a dim bulb, less lighthouse than vast sea with scattered bioluminescent glimmers. It is a cousin

Alchemist and homunculus

of the automaton, but whereas that kind of imposter-man, rebranded as a robot in the early twentieth century is built up out of parts metal, wooden, leather, by an inventor or tinkerer, a homunculus is concocted in a beaker, dish or alembic, and made to grow up slowly like a mould culture, a yogurt bacteria, a baby. The process borrows something from the biological realm, or perhaps, more precisely, steals it, mimicking by will and by artifice processes that are ordinarily supposed to unfold spontaneously and naturally, not by human intervention but by its absence.

May the dream of the alchemists, to produce artificial men, be said to have come true in any significant sense? Today, with beakers and similar such equipment, scientists can cause human ears to grow on the backs of mice; they can keep pig brains alive, and presumably thinking pig thoughts, even after the rest of their pig bodies have been carved up for meat; and they can edit the genome of a mosquito or a human being as if they were editing a Word file. In the beginning was the Word, writes the Apostle,

The 'earmouse'

which on one understanding is nothing other than the order that permeates nature and makes it into a unified, rational whole. For millennia, writing was conceived, by the minority of men who could do it and who were given to rhapsodising about it, as a variety of creation, *poiesis* (from which the word 'poetry' is derived), which duplicates as in a mirror the structure of the external world, of the reality, that writing is about.

John the Apostle

In the past few years we have witnessed the rise of the new and astoundingly powerful gene-splicing technology known as CRISPR/Cas9, which cuts right into a cell's genome at a given location and allows it to be edited as desired. And it is at just the same moment that poetry in the commonly understood sense is rapidly diminishing into a niche interest, like playing baroque music on period instruments, that we are at last witnessing the full unification of the work of the writer and the work of God: new beings are being written into existence, composed mostly in front of screens and on keyboards, and

that it is gene-splicing software we are running and not a tool from Microsoft seems a detail. Writing, at long last, really is creation.

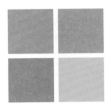

Microsoft logo

There are, however, as a genie would no doubt relish divulging immediately after granting us some remarkable new superpower, a couple of hitches. One is that we mortals still do not have the power of making anything out of nothing, but must always start with something pregiven, preformed, like the sourdough baker who begins with a yeast starter. But who started the starter? If we were to gain the power of a starterless start, this could only be in one of two ways: either by becoming fully divine creators of worlds out of nothing; or by collapsing the difference between the homunculus and the automaton, between that which is generated with a certain amount of external forcing, and that which is made through a simple rearrangement of parts. A machine can be made out of nothing, yet by the same token even when it exists it does not really exist,

A 12 volt car battery

not in the fullest sense, but is only a temporary assemblage. Cars and computers cannot die, except by analogy.

What really exists — what is, that is, a being, and not a mere thing — comes from something of its own kind that pre-exists it: its parents perhaps, or a seed, or a genetically identical mass from which it separates in the purest sort of reproduction there can be. We can splice, and engineer, and modify a pig, but we cannot bring a pig into being whole hog. The sort of writing that CRISPR/Cas9 makes possible, then, is not really the same as what we do when we open a blank Word file and get down to work, but rather it is as if we were given a prewritten text, and invited to cut-and-paste it into something new: the cut-up method, as William S. Burroughs — scion of a typewriter dynasty, and prophet of the imminent fusion of writing machines with living bodies — understood it.

William S. Burroughs

The other hitch, I am sorry to say, is that although we *can* do all this, we really, *really* should not be doing it. It was in the early 1800s that we moved from an old order in which there was something plainly diabolical about curiosity, in which the line between black magic and scientific experiment was not at all clear, to a brave new order of boundless progress. This was also the moment that gave voice to two of the most powerful cautionary tales of modern Prometheanism, two last swan-songs of the dying sense that nature must not be fully conquered and subordinated to our ends, that it is not ours, and that to come to believe otherwise was to give into a sort of temptation that in earlier times we were comfortable calling 'satanic'. In Germany, it was Goethe's 1829 play *Faust* that echoed the old warning; and in England, Mary Shelley's 1818 *Frankenstein: or, The Modern Prometheus.* 'The unhallowed arts' was how Shelley referred to the experimental sciences, to the conjuring up of nature's latent powers.

Faust raising the Devil

Dr Frankenstein's monster surely counts as a homunculus. He is not small, but he is dumb, and he comes into being from the starter material of a corpse, manipulated in stubborn, hubristic ignorance of all the good reasons not to proceed further. Certain elements of his creation by

Mary Shelley

the doctor, and of the doctor's creation by Shelley, place him squarely in his century: the author imagines that we might produce artificial life by use of freshly harnessed forces, notably galvanism and electricity, while two centuries earlier the alchemists preferred to speak of fermentation, a catch-all natural process that was invoked to explain a variety of phenomena that could not really be explained — the generation of animals, the production of heat in wet hay, the rotting of corpses, the alteration of grape juice into wine.

Galvanism of a frog

In his *De Natura Rerum* of 1537, the Swiss-German naturalist and physician commonly known as Paracelsus (1493–1541) offered a recipe for cooking up a little man. You are to take some human sperm, and seal it up in a cucurbit for forty days to make it putrefy; then you are to place it in a horse's womb, and nourish it with blood; and so on. The author claimed he tried the recipe, and that he obtained the desired results. The putrefaction is both what makes the homunculus possible, and what ensures he will never be a proper man, but only a little man, a counterfeit, soulless, semblance of a man. For true ensoulment can only happen within a human mother's womb, by divine intervention. Still, it is fitting and inevitable for men, in search of knowledge, thought Paracelsus, master of the unhallowed arts, to seek ever

to perfect the semblances they themselves create of God's work, to get ever closer to it, to the point that someday the two might be indistinguishable.

Now it is easy to mock Paracelsus's recommendations, in their details, but I insist they are not prima facie absurd. I myself, not too long ago, was charged with carrying a tube full of my own semen, extracted by not unpleasant means that I will not describe here and marked with a biohazard sticker, from a laboratory on one side of Paris to one on the other side, where it was then mixed in vitro with the preselected ovum of a certain cherished human. This effort was no more successful than Paracelsus's had been, and so all I have generated in this life have been words, pure words. But the fact that the anxious would-be parents of today are running from lab to lab in this way proves that Paracelsus was not wrong in any fundamental sense, and that the intervening centuries have only seen a refinement, and not a rejection, of his recipe. We use glass dishes and not horses' wombs for our artificial fertilisations, but such interspecies support is not wholly unknown in the way we manage our sexed bodies today —the urine of mares, for example, remains a key ingredient of oestrogen-replacement drugs.

Biohazard sticker

One might, again, go further and say that the alchemists were not wrong about anything, as most of their

MONSTERS 9 AND 10. GAIRA AND SANDA

Two beasts spawned from the discarded cells of Frankenstein's monster do battle with the Japanese military. The film is Ishirō Honda's *Furankenshutain no kaijū: Sanda tai Gaira* (*Frankenstein's Monsters: Sanda vs Gaira*) and the genre is *kaiju*, in which giant, near-invulnerable monsters lay waste to Japanese cities. *Kaiju*, pioneered by Honda, was among other things a response to the atom bomb detonations at Hiroshima and Nagasaki.

desiderata, the things they dared to dream of and to note down on their wish lists, have been realised in some form or other: as plastic, as nukes, and so on. These are of course monsters too. We think we are getting what we want, by manipulating the stuff of nature and releasing its latent powers, but again and again the plan backfires and our new creations come back to harm us, to choke the oceans and to make our safe homes as uninhabitable as the surfaces of stars. We know this is how things work, and we keep trying anyway.

US nuclear test

At present the ethics boards that approve research using gene-splicing assure us they are interested only in promoting salutary medical applications, and not in the creation of new immortalised germlines, that is, of cells that give rise to offspring that may then become part of a species' shared genetic profile. They aim to ameliorate our natural lives, by assisting nature in doing what it already does, and not to make nature itself artificial. Critics insist that if the technology is there, someone will eventually use it for ends the ethics boards decline to approve. And in any case our permanent alteration of nature is well under way, the monuments of it all around us, from the nitrogen cycle, to seedless grapes, to docile, neotenous farm animals. No ethics board ever approved the great majority of these transformations,

and opinions differ greatly as to which of them are beneficial, and which harmful.

Seedless grapes

The fear that animates myths such as *Frankenstein* is not of the power of our artifice itself, but of the power of nature which that artifice unleashes. A homunculus or a golem or a mandrake must, I have said, be dumb. For nature is dumb, not in the sense that it suffers from the sort of idiocy or cretinism or mental weaknesses our fellow human beings suffer from in varying degrees, but in the sense that it is insensitive to us, it does not listen to us, and so, once we have unleashed its latent powers, we cannot expect it to sympathise with our desperate pleas to spare us from their effects. Plastic and nuclear weapons are only further alterations of the stuff of nature, and will neither apologise nor mourn if they happen to serve as the means of our self-destruction.

Mandrake

What is particularly terrifying about the homunculus and all its relations and ancestors, as conceived in myth and in

Robocop

technology (not least the cyborg-humanoid law enforcer, whose arrival is only a matter of time), is that it is indifferent too, like plastic, like radioactivity, yet we can still, as if paradoxically, look it in the face. Naturally, our specialised face-perceiving occipital lobe supposes it has an 'in' here, something to work with, and so it scans the face in search of some sympathy. But a human brain is lighting up only on one side of this pairing, and it sees reflected back only a blank stare, blank as a corpse, mute as plastic, as indifferent to the reasonings of an ethics board as the star-force packed into a nuclear warhead. The monsters we have created are all around us, but the most terrifying of them are the ones we have made in our likeness. *Homunculi quam similes turpissima nobis monstra*, to adapt an old remark first made in reference to monkeys. It is because they are so similar to us that homunculi are the ugliest of monsters.

JUSTIN E. H. SMITH is an editor-at-large of *Cabinet magazine* and the author, most recently, of *Irrationality: A History of the Dark Side of Reason*. He lives in Paris, where he regularly visits Étienne and Isidore Geoffroy Saint Hilaire's teratological collection at the Galerie d'Anatomie Comparée, and always feels a tug of sympathy for the cyclops pig fetus and the two-headed lamb.

BABY

JEAN HANNAH EDELSTEIN, due quite soon, doesn't know who she is making, or who they will make her into.

MONSTER 11. MY CHILD

I was halfway through my first prenatal yoga class when I scanned the room of my fellow pregnant women performing Warrior 2. I looked at all of them, ripe and round in their maternity yoga outfits, I breathed out deeply, and I thought to myself, 'What a shame for all of these women that they are having babies that won't be as good as mine.' And then I thought, 'I'm a monster!'

I had, of course, no grounds for such a self-aggrandising belief in the superiority of my nascent offspring, except that I will be that baby's mother. Except that being a mother is the strongest justification of all. Pregnancy will do that to you, or at least my pregnancy has: made me a person who is in some way so self-involved that I've come to believe that producing a child made in my own image is justified, as if I am in possession of some kind of omnipotence. As if I am so important as to be deserving of replication, to exert that highest of powers. God made man in His own image. Why shouldn't I?

And yet. As I lie on my side on the sofa of an early-third-trimester evening — the best position in which to lie to reduce the effects of this small person growing and thumping inside me, the punches and kicks, the pressure the small body places on my sciatic nerve, sending shooting pains down my leg — of course it crosses my mind that I may be incorrect. What if my baby is not the best baby? What if this occupant of my body — this additional being that I'm carrying with me everywhere I go — turns out to be some kind of monster itself? What if the punches and kicks are not cute, but a sign of the pain to come?

Like all parents, I take prophylactic measures against the worst case scenario. I read books about parenting, instructions about how to raise your child with total smothering focus or benevolent, regimented abandonment. Each promises to result in a child that is a kind of perfection, a road map through the labyrinth that should leave parent and child unscathed. Dr Jekyll, Jekyll junior. Each book suggests that the other will lead to certain disaster: wrong turns, confrontation, battles that drain you of life and turn you into your worst self.

I'm afraid. Of course I am. I regard children on the street who behave like angels, and think, 'My child will be like that, surely that's what I have to look forward to.'

But then I regard children on the street who behave like demons, and think, 'My child could, let's be honest, be like that.'

I eat a salad and think, 'This meal will infuse my offspring with the kind of vitamins necessary for an exemplary life.' I eat a bagel with too much cream cheese, check that no one is looking before I messily wipe smudges of it off my mouth with the back of my hand, and think, 'What if this sandwich has ruined the baby?' I don't really believe that a single lunch could be the cause of monstrosity. And yet I don't feel entirely sure that it could not.

2. WARRIOR 2

Popular pose. Bent front knee, straight back leg, arms extended in a straight line to the sides.

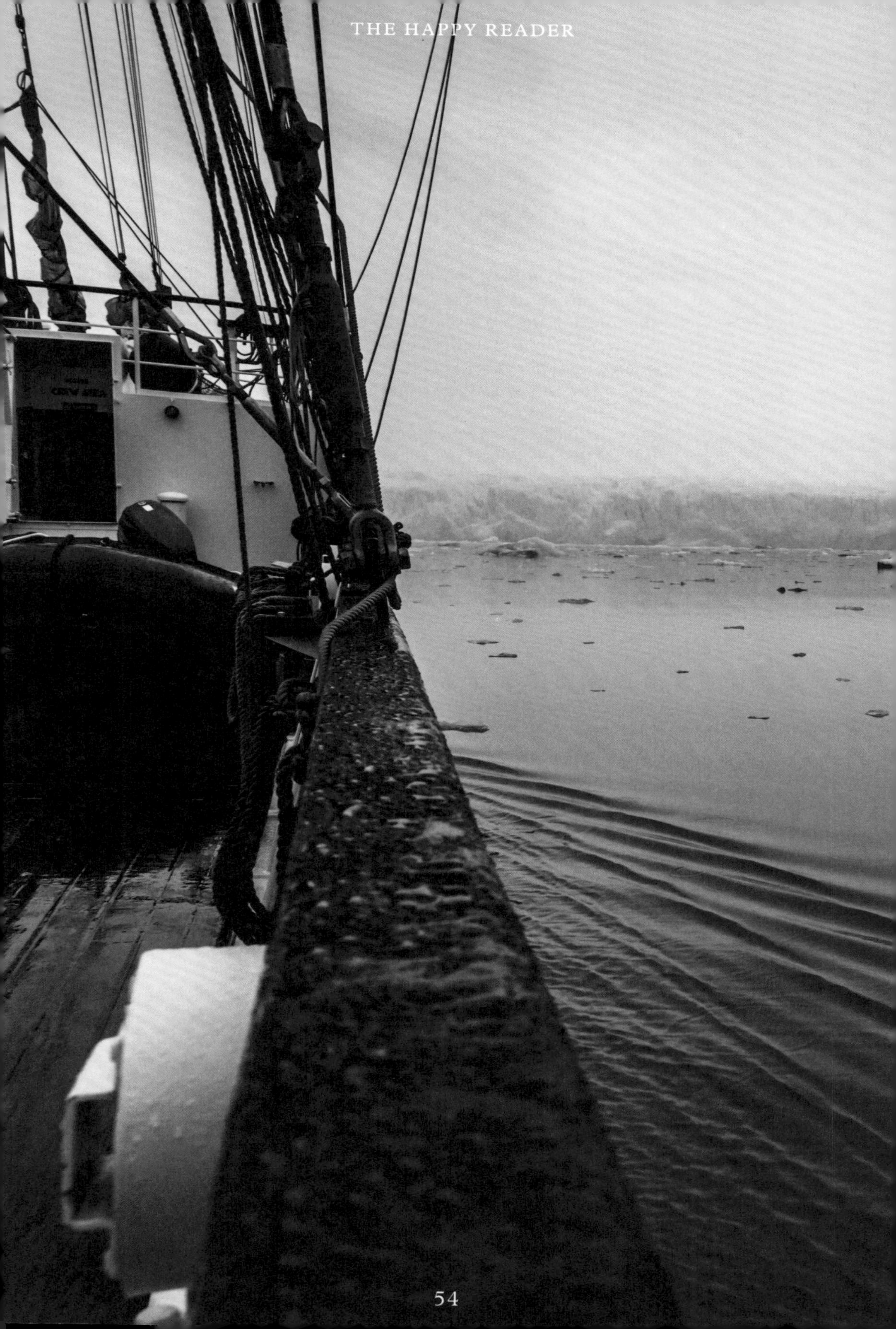

MONSTER 12. ARCTIC CIRCLE

'A sledge... had drifted towards us in the night on a large fragment of ice. Only one dog remained alive; but there was a human being within it.' The Arctic Sea, canvas for the first and last chapters of Shelley's novel as well as our own calamitous climate change monster, are here photographed by IAN FRIED... AIDER during sail's permission to Scalloped North

At times, I'm sure of it, every child is a monster — every single one of us. One day I will look at my child and think, 'You're the worst, and it's all my fault.' As with all of the most terrifying monsters, the greatest fear in becoming a mother is in anticipation of the unknown: the unknowable secrets that lie on the other side of the horizon. The heavy silences that are waiting to be filled. In time, all that I do know for sure is that this being will tear its way out of my body — on its own volition, or with the assistance of doctors — and come roaring and thrashing into the light. When I behold the face of my potential little monster for the first time, I'll weep, I'm sure I will. In part because no matter what else happens, there's no turning back: it will be unleashed. And I'll be looking at something of myself.

JEAN HANNAH EDELSTEIN is a writer who lives in Brooklyn — and yes, it rhymes with 'Frankenstein'. Her new book, *This Really Isn't About You*, is about her, and out now.

PLAYLIST

A mini-mixtape by JEREMY ALLEN of songs that are created, and then regretted, and then pursue their creators everywhere in a humiliating trap that only death can assuage.

MONSTERS 13–17. CREATIVE REGRET

A FLOCK OF SEAGULLS — 'I Ran (So Far Away)' (1982)
The Liverpool synth-pop four-piece couldn't have envisaged the eternal derision they'd endure for sporting haircuts that resembled deluged shop awnings. Singer Mike Score's anguish also stemmed from a bewilderment that their fourth single had stormed nearly every chart in the world, but wasn't as accomplished as successive singles that weren't nearly as well received. 'Every time I perform live, everyone just wants to hear "I Ran",' he lamented when interviewed. 'I'm sick of it!'

SERGEI RACHMANINOFF — 'Prelude in C# minor' (1892)
The famous piano composition was simply known by the diminutive 'The Prelude' to Sergei Rachmaninov's fans, such was its popularity, but the man who wrote it was tortured by the adulation it provoked. In an interview with the *Minneapolis Tribune* in 1921, he grumbled: 'I am often sorry I wrote it. I can never, never escape from a concert hall without playing it. It pursues me everywhere.'

THE WOMBLES — 'The Wombling Song' (1973)
'The Wombles have been a bit of a bête noire,' music industry impresario Mike Batt confessed in 2008. 'Before the Wombles, I was making a living as an arranger, doing credible stuff.' The musician, songwriter and record producer had become head of A&R at Liberty Records as a nineteen-year-old; at twenty-three he was asked to write

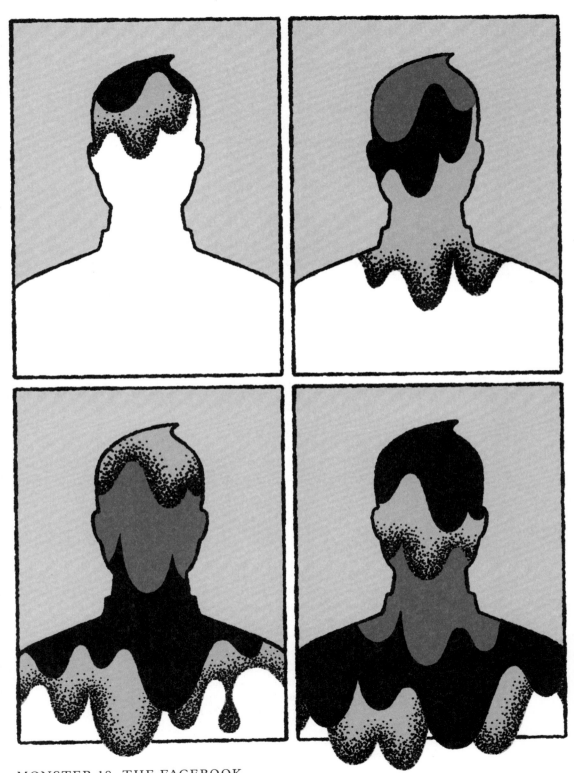

MONSTER 18. THE FACEBOOK
Does Mark Zuckerberg feel like Victor Frankenstein? His creation, which once seemed like such harmless fun, is coming for us all. Illustration by LAN TRUONG.

the theme song to a children's TV programme, a turning point that would lead to a lifelong association. 'I did strings for Traffic. Even John Peel used to pop round to see what I was up to. Always pre-Womble. Post-Womble, I never heard from him again.'

LED ZEPPELIN — 'Stairway to Heaven' (1971)

In 1988, Robert Plant told *Rolling Stone* he'd 'break out in hives' if he had to sing 'Stairway to Heaven' every night. 'I wrote those lyrics and found that song to be of some importance and consequence in 1971.' Whereas now? 'I don't know. It's just not for me.' The most revered eight minutes in heavy rock by the fourth-bestselling music act of all time it might be, but to the Black Country-born rocker it was still 'that bloody wedding song'.

THE PRETENDERS — 'Brass In Pocket' (1979)

Chrissie Hynde told producer Chris Thomas that 'Brass in Pocket' would be released over her dead body. The third single from The Pretenders' self-titled debut album went to number one and made Hynde a household name. 'Was it pop? Motown? Rock? It didn't seem to know what it was,' she told *Classic Rock*. 'I used to cringe when I heard my voice on those early Pretenders recordings, and then that fucker went to number one! I remember walking around Oxford Circus hearing it blasting out of people's radios. I was mortified.'

JEREMY ALLEN is a music and culture journalist. Whilst visiting that monstrous city of Geneva he recently broke a crown on an unyielding baguette.

ARNIE

The monster enthusiast and art critic CHARLIE FOX excavates a single momentous freeze-frame from *Terminator 2*.

MONSTER 19. THAT TERMINATOR

INTERVIEWER: Do you visualise yourself as a living sculpture?
ARNOLD SCHWARZENEGGER: Yes, definitely. Good body-builders have the same mind when it comes to sculpture that a sculptor has.
— *Pumping Iron* (1977)

'Who are you?' asks the scientist Miles Dyson, halfway through James Cameron's epic *Terminator 2: Judgment Day* (1991). By way of explanation, the T-800 (Arnold Schwarzenegger) cuts into the Mr Universe muscles in the lower half of his arm to reveal the chrome skeleton underneath. Minds melt. He is a cyborg, and he is terrifying. He beholds the trippy magnificence of his own body for a moment as if freeze-framed. There's something beautiful about this eerie sculptural tableau, too. A ton of data is encrypted in that image: the bionic arms of Desert Storm veterans (the first Gulf War kicked off the year *T2* hit theatres), the ghoulish details seen in classical paintings (look at

Arnold Schwarzenegger in *Terminator 2*.

the juicy tendons exposed in Rembrandt's 1632 painting *The Anatomy Lesson of Dr Nicolaes Tulp*) and, *natürlich*, Frankenstein's monster. 'Child, what is the meaning of this?' the monster asks a little kid in the woods halfway through Shelley's novel. Nearly two hundred years later, John Connor (Edward Furlong), his counterpart and the cute punk that the T-800 must protect, offers the best answer: 'This is *deep*.'

If you're a monster, your body is prone to freaky and brain-melting disturbances. Natalie Portman gasps as she plucks that spooky feather from her body in *Black Swan* (2010) and David Naughton howls in *An American Werewolf in London* (1981) as his hand deforms into a lycanthrope's paw. But when the T-800 exposes the futuristic bones underneath, the vibe warps. The body zoning out over its own monstrous oddity was never human anyway. It doesn't scream, it just stares. Call the lab. (It feels like a weird omen that three big box office hits the year I was born — *Terminator 2*, *Beauty and the Beast* and *The Silence of the Lambs*, which occupied top, third and fifth place in end-of-year totals — show you how to befriend, and sometimes love, a monster.)

Like Shelley's novel, James Cameron's movies are cautionary tales about the dangers and delights of playing with technology. The extended version of *The Abyss* (1989) climaxes with aliens showing Ed Harris a sizzle reel of military destruction. *Titanic* (1997) is about the *Titanic*. Prometheus, the daredevil who steals fire from the gods and suffers awful punishment for the feat, is always somewhere in the background (*Frankenstein* famously retells his tale in 'modern' form according to the book's subtitle). Prometheus' endlessly regenerating liver feasted on by hungry vultures is the earliest example of artificial-tissue engineering. It's <u>Cronenberg</u> in antiquity. But this moment from *Terminator 2* is about having flesh and knowing it will rot: death and self-consciousness, I guess, aka the two inextricable mind-fucks of human existence.

Only Arnold Schwarzenegger, with his robot affect and classical physique, could sell the paradox of a machine troubled by this problem. *Terminator 2* is about a cyborg becoming human but it's also another

3. CRONENBERG
—
'Everybody's a mad scientist, and life is their lab. We're all trying to experiment to find a way to live.' — David Cronenberg, whose films include *Eastern Promises* (2007) and *The Fly* (1986).

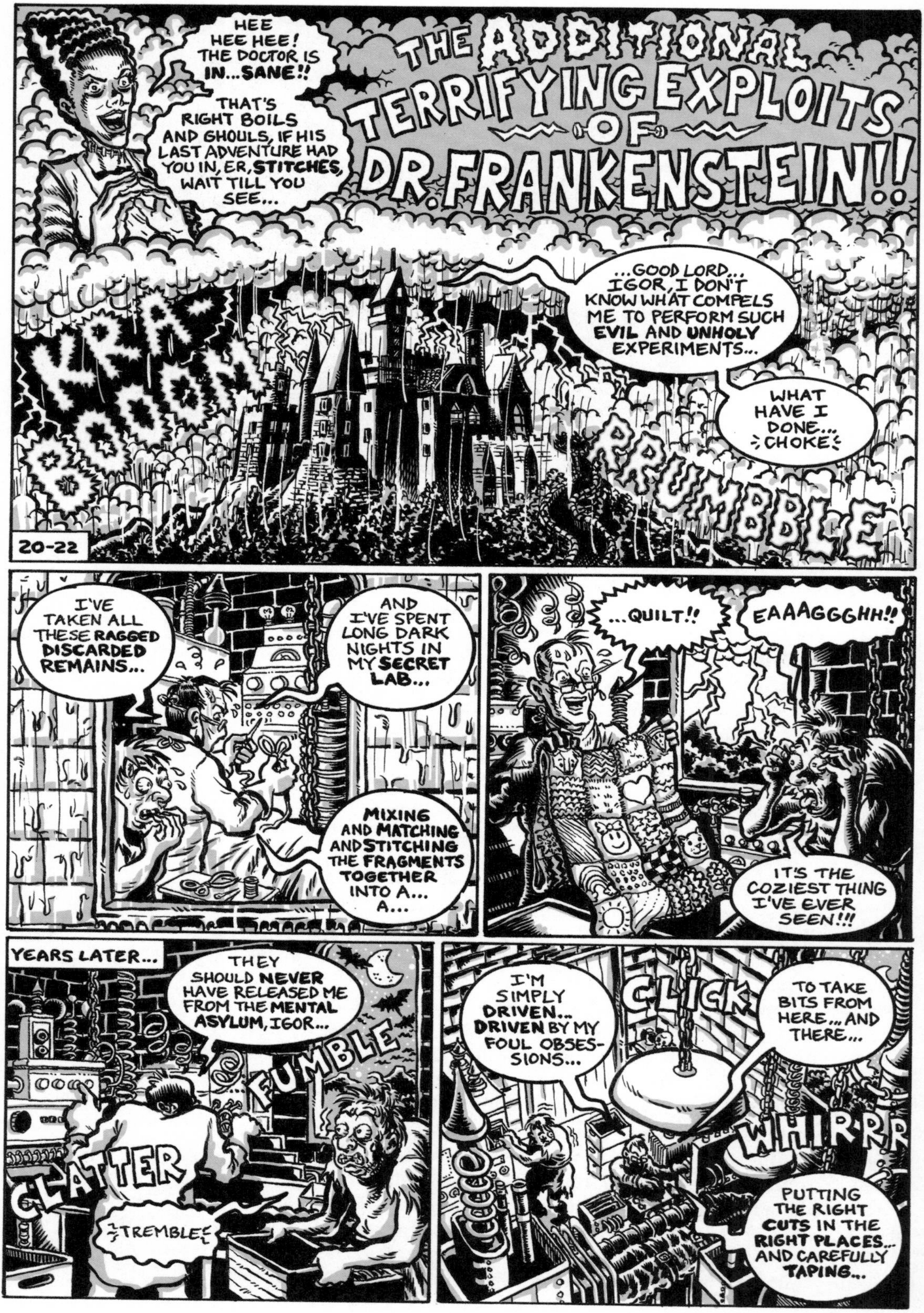
HEE HEE HEE! THE DOCTOR IS IN... SANE!!
THAT'S RIGHT BOILS AND GHOULS, IF HIS LAST ADVENTURE HAD YOU IN, ER, STITCHES, WAIT TILL YOU SEE...
THE ADDITIONAL TERRIFYING EXPLOITS OF DR. FRANKENSTEIN!!
KRA-BOOOM!
...GOOD LORD... IGOR, I DON'T KNOW WHAT COMPELS ME TO PERFORM SUCH EVIL AND UNHOLY EXPERIMENTS...
WHAT HAVE I DONE... CHOKE
RRUMBBLE
20-22
I'VE TAKEN ALL THESE RAGGED DISCARDED REMAINS...
AND I'VE SPENT LONG DARK NIGHTS IN MY SECRET LAB...
MIXING AND MATCHING AND STITCHING THE FRAGMENTS TOGETHER INTO A... A...
...QUILT!!
EAAAGGGHH!!
IT'S THE COZIEST THING I'VE EVER SEEN!!!
YEARS LATER...
THEY SHOULD NEVER HAVE RELEASED ME FROM THE MENTAL ASYLUM, IGOR...
FUMBLE
CLATTER
TREMBLE
I'M SIMPLY DRIVEN... DRIVEN BY MY FOUL OBSESSIONS...
CLICK
TO TAKE BITS FROM HERE... AND THERE...
WHIRRR
PUTTING THE RIGHT CUTS IN THE RIGHT PLACES... AND CAREFULLY TAPING...

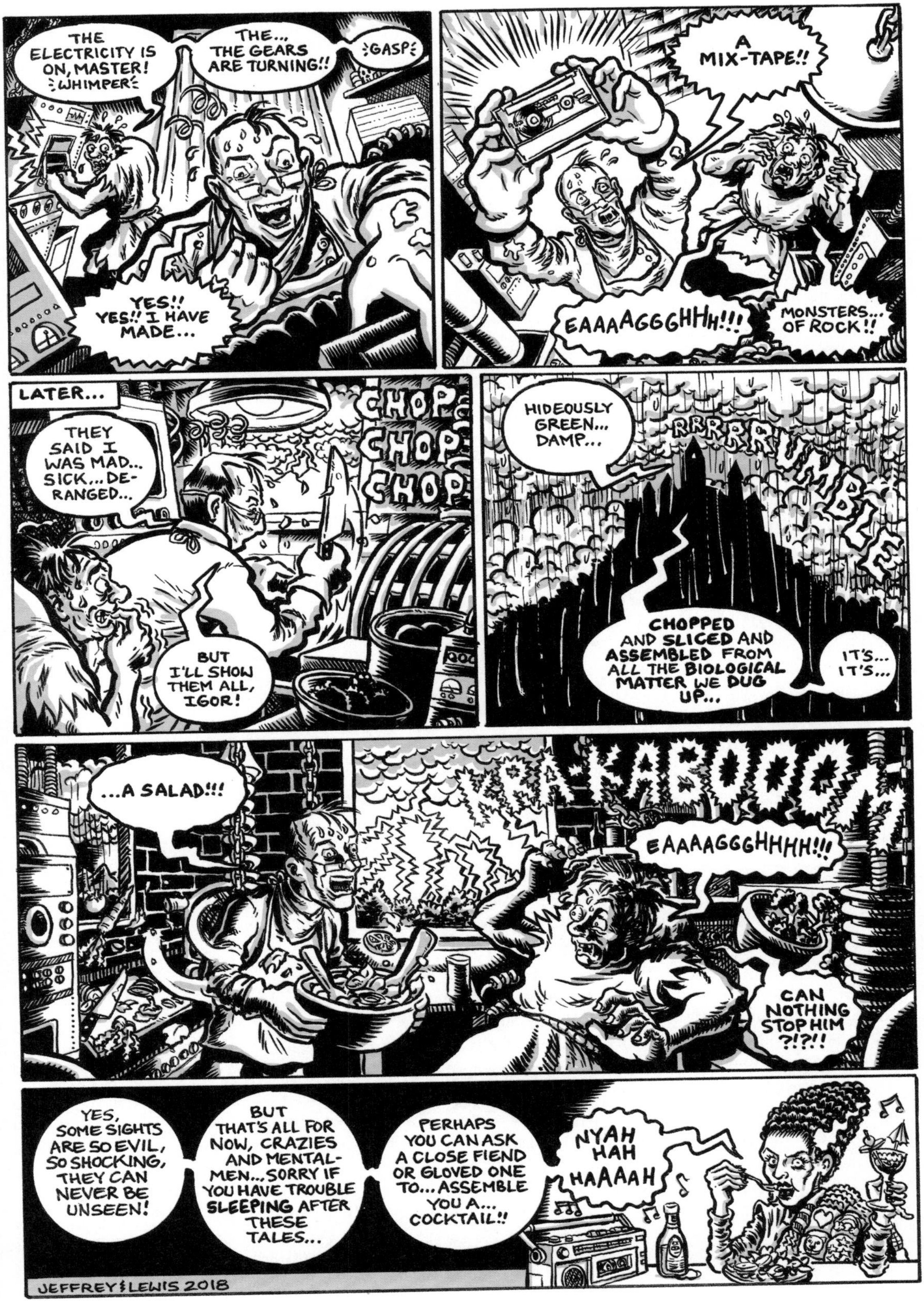
THE ELECTRICITY IS ON, MASTER! WHIMPER
THE..., THE GEARS ARE TURNING!!
GASP
YES!! YES!! I HAVE MADE...
A MIX-TAPE!!
EAAAAGGGHHH!!!
MONSTERS... OF ROCK!!
LATER...
THEY SAID I WAS MAD... SICK... DE-RANGED...
CHOP CHOP CHOP
BUT I'LL SHOW THEM ALL, IGOR!
HIDEOUSLY GREEN... DAMP...
RRRRRUMBLE
CHOPPED AND SLICED AND ASSEMBLED FROM ALL THE BIOLOGICAL MATTER WE DUG UP...
IT'S... IT'S...
...A SALAD!!!
KRA-KABOOOM
EAAAAGGGHHHH!!!
CAN NOTHING STOP HIM ?!?!!
YES, SOME SIGHTS ARE SO EVIL, SO SHOCKING, THEY CAN NEVER BE UNSEEN!
BUT THAT'S ALL FOR NOW, CRAZIES AND MENTAL-MEN... SORRY IF YOU HAVE TROUBLE SLEEPING AFTER THESE TALES...
PERHAPS YOU CAN ASK A CLOSE FIEND OR GLOVED ONE TO... ASSEMBLE YOU A... COCKTAIL!!
NYAH HAH HAAAAH
JEFFREY LEWIS 2018

instalment from the peculiar history of Arnie presenting himself as inhuman. Read his Pygmalion thoughts on the sculptural power of the body from the documentary *Pumping Iron*. Or rewatch him being Mr Freeze in Joel Schumacher's zany masterpiece *Batman & Robin* (1997), an 'ice-man' who keeps his dead wife in a refrigerated vitrine. The father of this zombie performance style is Boris Karloff in *Franken-stein* (1931): stomping, monosyllabic, 'sorta alive outside' — like John Connor says — but dead within.

Weird daddy questions recur. Victor Frankenstein longs to create life so 'no father could claim the gratitude of his child as completely as I should deserve theirs.' But biology is a problem (think of John Connor's mother, Sarah, screaming at Miles Dyson the cyborg scientist: 'You don't know what it's like [...] to create a life, to feel it growing inside you') so he dredges matter from the 'unhallowed damps of the grave' and creates a zombie. (Arnie will take on the the Victor-esque role of a scientist too when he plays the world's first pregnant man in Ivan Reitman's 1994 goofball comedy *Junior*). In the same spirit as the monster chasing Victor, the T-800 has come back from the future to haunt Dyson, his own 'accursed creator', who hasn't even invented him yet.

Scan the picture again for extra microcosmic detail, like the T-800 using his complex operating system to understand his environment— target acquired. Arnie's melancholy stance is more Hamlet mid-so-liloquy than Hercules at a muscle contest. Since he's on a mission to assure his own obsolescence, maybe staring at his skeleton draws the T-800 into the same questions about death that occupy the prince when he eyeballs Yorick's skull. The end awaits. Since he can't commit suicide, the T-800 is lowered into a vat of molten steel, half his own metal skull exposed through his scarred organic simulation of a face: a memento mori for Generation X. The show-and-tell with the arm was a warm-up act for that big farewell.

I was going to fade out with something gloomy about the relation-ship between *Terminator 2* and *E.T.* (a non-human angel protects a troubled boy) but then the ghosts of the Romantics reminded me of the sublime. The arm scene is the first example of twenty-first-centu-ry sublime in my brain: a mind-boggling awe kindled by the strange relationship between humans and simulations of reality. File it along-side the shimmying psychedelic particularities of green and purple hairs that create Sully's fur in *Monsters, Inc.* (2001) or the first-person experience of your shadowy drug-dealing avatar's death in *Enter the Void* (2009). I am the same age as *Terminator 2*. I remember the hot suburban night of my eighth birthday when I watched a VHS tape of the movie after mutating myself into a hyperactive demon thanks to a nervous system overloaded by Haribo and a purple Game Boy Colour — the translucent body let you see its insides, too. I remember the feeling of scary, sky-high wonder hitting me when I saw the beautiful skeleton arm and making the sublime's trademark noise: '*Whoa...*'

London-based writer CHARLIE FOX is the author of the essay collection *This Young Monster*, a celebration of artists and other characters who raise hell, transform their bodies and anger their elders, ranging from *Alice in Wonderland* to Leigh Bowery and Harmony Korine.

MONSTER 23. BORIS KARLOFF
'Feminine fans seem to get some sort of emotional kick out of this sublimation of the bed-time ghost story,' puzzled *Variety* in its assessment of 1931's *Frankenstein*. In the end, Boris Karloff's mute, neck-bolted monster (nothing like Shelley's verbose long-haired original) became the archetypal synthetic human. But it's easy to forget how unsettlingly odd he was — how sad, how innocent, and how brutal.

WHO IS FRANKENSTEIN?

MOST PEOPLE DO CONFUSE HIM
WITH HIS MONSTER.
SLEEP OF REASON PRODUCES
MONSTERS.
THESE MONSTERS DESTROY OUR
CULTURE.

FRANKENSTEIN IS THE
PERSONIFICATION OF PASSION.

LETTERS

A former cover star reminisces, and a decades-old
art project is welcomed.

Dear Seb,

When I heard about your intention to dedicate an issue of *The Happy Reader* to *Frankenstein*, I remembered a print I made back in 1991 as part of *491*, a kind of gothic, underground black and white fanzine published in Barcelona by the Real Art Foundation. The portfolio included references to monsters and 'monstresses' of all kinds, and my contribution was a tribute (see left) to the figure of Frankenstein's monster, a short poem illustrated by an image taken from a German expressionist movie. Having a look at it now, after all these years, it really has this eighties/nineties nostalgic look, which fits the protagonist's aura. I hope you like it.

Erich Weiss
Barcelona

Dear The Happy Reader,

I always finish *The Happy Reader* with a fulsome to-be-read list. I'd like to thank cover star Olly Alexander for substantially increasing its length in the last issue – particularly his recommendation of *Dancer from the Dance* by Andrew Holleran, a previously unheard of cult classic.

Dancer from the Dance dropped me straight into the gay community of New York City in the 1970s, written with the kind of detail that you'd only get if you'd been part of that scene – from the extravagant fashion ensembles to the funk soundtrack. While I enjoyed the spike-heel sharp satire, on reading it in 2018, I couldn't help but romanticise the sweaty nightclub scenes, the endless days and nights of longing. Perhaps it's because it's pre-AIDS, perhaps it's because New York seems so different now, or perhaps it's

because I, like many of the book's characters, suffer from nostalgia for things that can never quite be...

I've been listening to the soundtrack to *Dancer from the Dance* on repeat (fellow fans have compiled the songs mentioned in the book as Spotify playlists) and, as I'm writing this, the lyrics to Patti Jo's 'Make Me Believe in You' are still running around my head: 'Make me believe in you / Show me your love can be true'. Despite actually spending my summer in a sanitised London, part of my heart has stayed in 1970s New York.

Sincerely,
Frances Ambler
London

Dear Seb,

A note on *Frankenstein* — my abiding memory of preparing and recording it for 2013's audiobook was how I was sure I had read and knew it, having made a TV movie of it in Slovakia years before, and yet how different it felt this time around: how bitterly hopeful and sad and not-at-all scary the creature is, and how utterly terrifyingly the human monster of ambition looms. When the creature speaks it is so articulate and beautiful it seemed to me the saddest sound in the world.

Dan Stevens
Los Angeles

It's a thrill to be published, so don't delay! Send correspondences in an email to letters@thehappyreader.com or in an old-fangled envelope to The Happy Reader, Penguin Books, 80 Strand, London WC2R 0RL.

Warm up for the next issue of *The Happy Reader* by reading summer 2019's Book of the Season. Subscribe and purchase back issues at thehappyreader.com

AURELIUS TIME, SELF TIME

In a world swamped by brilliantly effective distractions, the question 'what is actually important?' feels at once urgent and baffling. Can it be an unrelated coincidence that Marcus Aurelius' *Meditations*, our Book of the Season for summer 2019, is flying off the shelves? That it's doing so almost two thousand years after being written, and despite our living in a world that its author, the last of Rome's so-called 'good emperors', could never have imagined, is testament to the clarity and essential simplicity of the wisdom it contains. Marcus Aurelius — known as 'the Philosopher' — was emperor of Rome from AD 161 to AD 180. These reflections were written not for publication, but as personal memos for self-improvement: an alternative title is *The Communings with Himself of Marcus Aurelius*.

Meditations is an important work of Stoic philosophy, and it's one of the oldest books that can be filed under 'self-help'. Take it on holiday. Read it on the train. It can be read cover to cover, or by repeatedly opening at random, for a few seconds at a time, contemplating wisdoms such as, 'If your distress has some external cause, it is not the thing itself that troubles you, but your own judgment of it — and you can erase this immediately.' The next instalment of *The Happy Reader* will be published in June 2019; readers are encouraged to mull over Marcus Aurelius' private thoughts before then.

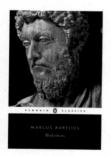

Jacket for *Meditations*, originally written from 161 to 180 AD.